SWIPE RIGHT FOR ROMANCE

A LOVE BUG NOVEL
BOOK 1

KELLY COLLINS

CHAPTER ONE

JUNIE

The morning sun peeks through the curtains like a nosy neighbor, spotlighting my empty bed. Oh, the irony. I'm the genius behind Love Bug, the app that's supposed to make Cupid look like an amateur with a slingshot. My app promises love so intense it could make a cactus cry, yet here I am, cuddling with my cold, unresponsive sheets. It's like being a personal trainer and tripping over your own shoelaces.

My mind takes a stroll down ex-boyfriend lane, a sad parade of men who were more caricature than character. Think guys who live in their mom's basement, their mismatched socks screaming, "I've given up!" Men who think romance can flourish amidst the aroma of microwaved pizza rolls and the glow of video games. At this point, I'm less of a love guru and more of a bug zapper for the romantically challenged.

But today? Today is different. I've got a meeting with someone who could be the fairy godmother to my

Cinderella story, the venture capitalist to my start-up dreams. If this goes well, Love Bug will be more than just a pipe dream and a tax write-off. And maybe, just maybe, I'll find someone who doesn't think "Netflix and chill" is a long-term relationship plan.

So here I am, eyes sparkling like a kid in a candy store, and "swipe right for romance" is practically my new catchphrase. I'm all set for my meeting, armed with Love Bug—the app that's going to make Cupid file for unemployment. Seriously, who wouldn't want to invest in love's next big thing?

I catch a glimpse of myself in the mirror and flash a grin. I'm rocking my lucky shorts, the ones that saved me from becoming a human speed bump. Liv, my bestie, and guardian angel, yanked me back by my belt loop just as a bus was about to introduce me to the afterlife. I walk through my apartment, my pink fuzzy socks generating enough static to power a small village. I enter the kitchen, where the aroma of coffee promises a day that's all sunshine, lollipops, and zero dread.

"Ah, my liquid courage," I say, grabbing my mug that boldly declares, "Turning Mere Mortals Into Morning Avengers!" A dollop of oat milk and a dash of vanilla later, my coffee morphs into an elixir that could probably give Popeye a run for his money.

Mug in hand, I sashay to my desk like I'm about to accept an Oscar, ready to conquer whatever challenges today throws at me. My laptop wakes up with a cheerful hum, as if it's just as excited about today as I am. As it springs to life, I take a moment to admire my apartment. I have a futon that's more colorful than a Mardi Gras parade, and a chunky blanket that's practically begging for a rom-com binge. My place is a delightful mess, the physical manifestation of my creative soul.

My walls are a veritable "Who's Who" of visionaries—Musk, Jobs, Winfrey. They're like my silent life coaches, always there to remind me, "Hey, if we can do it, so can you, but no pressure, okay?" My whiteboard is a chaotic swirl of scribbles and arrows that only make sense to me —and maybe a psychic on a good day.

My desk is its own landscape of crumpled notes and unpaid bills, each one screaming, "This meeting better go well, or else!" I've already played the ol' switcheroo with the utility companies—sending the electric bill to the gas company and vice versa. At this point, they're probably on to me.

I'm on the brink of a financial free fall, contemplating pawning my grandmother's wedding set. More than just jewelry, it represents the enduring love my grandparents shared for 55 years. Now, it rests in my nightstand, a silent testament to the love story I've yet to find. Each time I open that drawer, memories of Sundays at their house flood back—smelling the aroma of baked bread and hearing their cherished tales of meeting, enduring challenges, and sharing joys. My grandfather would often glance at my grandmother and whisper, "All because of these rings and our promises." They symbolize more than metal and stone. They are a legacy of love and a reminder of everything I desire. It will crush me if I have to let them go, but what choice do I have if this goes poorly? Grandma would turn in her grave if I was homeless.

Coffee in hand, I lock eyes with my laptop screen. Love Bug has bugs that need squashing and potential that's begging to be unleashed. I'm ready, armed with caffeine, dreams, and the stubbornness of a fire ant that refuses to be stepped on.

Just then, my phone buzzes, shattering my focus. It's a text from Liv.

Ready to roll ... I mean, scroll?

Ah, Liv, the pun queen and the artistic genius behind Love Bug's look and feel.

I flex my fingers and shoot a message back.

Let's create a buzz the world can't ignore.

It's cheesy, but it makes me smile.

I'm here.

Seconds later she bursts through the door, arms laden with kombucha and vegan cookies from Pies Before Guys. Because, priorities, right?

Liv's entrance is so grand, she could give any Broadway star a run for their money. "Brain fuel," she announces, setting down her haul like it's a treasure chest of pirate gold.

And just like that, we're ready. Ready to pitch, ready to dazzle, and more than ready to turn Love Bug into the next big thing in romance. So, world, you better watch out. We're here to make love happen, one swipe at a time.

I crack open a kombucha, grinning at Liv. "You're the best."

"I know," she says, eyeing me like a fashion police officer about to make an arrest. "Juniper Lee Parker, you're not seriously wearing that, are you?"

I glance down at my T-shirt, which proudly declares, "I'm not weird. I'm a limited edition."

"What's the issue?" I ask.

Liv's eyes do a full 360. "Would you wear that to a job interview? Because this is basically that."

The meeting is important to Liv because the investor is a friend of a friend of her father's and has ties to their family in Japan. But I bet, just like every other investor, he'll glance at the app and dash, exactly like the last seven did. *Here we go again.*

"Maybe we're interviewing him too. What if he's a dud?" I ask.

Liv grabs my arm and drags me back to my room. "If he's got cash and is willing to part with it, he's Prince Charming in my book. Now, why the limited-edition get-up?"

I sigh. "Ran out of detergent. Turns out water alone doesn't quite do the trick."

Liv shakes her head. "You're a hot mess."

"I prefer digital wizard," I say, smirking. "Besides, I'm sure I look better than anything Ethan would cobble together."

"If Ethan were on this call, I'd raid his closet too, but he's not. He's probably in his basement coding the next big thing. Guys like him only come up for air and donuts," Liv says, dragging me into my room and diving into my wardrobe. She surfaces with a red shirt and a black sweater. Add some antennae, and I'd be a walking, talking Love Bug mascot.

"Okay, but the lucky shorts stay," I insist.

"Fine, just keep your butt in the chair during the call so he can't see them," Liv says.

"Deal."

Liv dashes back to the living room, fussing over the decor like it's a set for a Hollywood movie.

"Do you think he cares about the throw pillows?"

"We can't risk it," she says, eyeing my shorts one last time. As always, she's right. We can't risk anything, so I retreat back to my room to change into some respectable black slacks—my funeral pants, as I like to call them.

"We've got five minutes," she calls out.

I re-emerge, now fully pants-clad.

Liv grins. "That's the spirit." She pops open her kombucha as we dial into the call. The room is thick with anticipation.

The screen flickers, and there's Mr. Morimoto, all the way from Kotohira, Japan, dressed in a suit that screams "I mean business." I suddenly appreciate Liv's fashion intervention. I steal a look at her, decked out in Chanel. Slyly, I shift my chair, spotlighting her and letting shadows claim me.

After the customary bows and greetings, Liv takes a deep breath and kicks off our pitch. "Good afternoon, Mr. Morimoto. Shall we dive into the future of romance?"

She gets right to it. "Love Bug isn't just another app where you swipe left so much you develop carpal tunnel. We're in the business of making meaningful connections based on shared interests, unique quirks, and the kind of conversations that don't involve 'What's your sign?'"

She nudges me under the table, her heel accidentally stepping on my toe, a clear hint to jump in. Trying to hide the sudden jolt of pain, I lean forward, catching my water glass just before it topples over. Regaining my composure, I clear my throat awkwardly. "You know," I start, my voice slightly higher than I intend, "online dating these days can be ... um ... disheartening?" I muster a nervous laugh.

Pulling out my phone in a flustered haste, I accidentally open my camera app, quickly flashing an unflattering double-chin selfie to the room. "Oops! Wrong app," I mumble. Once I find the correct photos, I continue, "Look at these profile pics from the popular dating apps. They've got more filters and edits than a big-budget movie. But then when these people meet in person?" I pause for effect. "They realize they've been sold a fantasy. It's all surface, no depth. More about that perfect shot than a genuine connection. Where's the authenticity? The real, raw, awkward beauty of getting to know someone?"

"Love Bug sifts through the superficial to focus on what truly counts—compatibility over catfishing," Liv continues, beaming. "We're not just changing the game. We're rewriting the rulebook."

Silence hangs in the virtual room, but Liv isn't deterred.

"Our compatibility quiz, crafted by our in-house love guru Junie, is as engaging as a rom-com, not a slog through a tax form," she says. "And our graphics? Think Pixar, not PowerPoint."

I fumble a bit before interjecting, "Uh, so instead of, you know, those typical flashy profile pics, we've got ... um, avatars! They kinda show the real you but in a digital, fun way." I hold up my phone but nearly drop it. "Okay, see this little fire ant here? That's supposed to be me." I giggle nervously. "Determined and all that."

"You think a fire ant is sexy?" he asks.

"Well, it's not the bug that's hot, it's the traits it represents," I say, trying to keep my cool. "Think of it as the spirit animal of dating."

"Who wants to date an ant? Especially one that bites?" Mr. Morimoto fires back, clearly missing the point.

"Let me explain." I take a deep breath and lean over so he can see me more clearly on the screen. "You kick things off with a questionnaire that delves deep, mapping out the intricacies of your inner workings. It's more than your favorite color or the name of your first pet. It's the essence of you, laid bare for the algorithms to play matchmaker based on your personalities. Then, only if the stars of compatibility align, do they factor in the miles between you. It's no good finding your soul mate if they're from another continent, right?

Once you're cozied up in that sweet spot of mutual interest, the game changes—it's challenge time. But not your run-of-the-mill truth or dare. No, these are personalized, crafted to carve out paths for deeper connections. Perhaps you'll both find yourselves sipping lattes at the same quirky bookstore cafe, unknowingly brushing hands as you reach for the same dog-eared copy of 'Love in the Time of Cholera.' Or maybe it's a scavenger hunt where each clue unravels a layer of your life story. Sometimes the questions are the same and sometimes they're different. It could be that one of you gets a question and the other may not, but that's the algorithm in the background fine-tuning the match. Because you don't know by sight who your match could be, you become more attuned to your surroundings, the potential in every glance, every smile-alive in the present, inadvertently shaping yourself into a better match for whoever's heart is about to sync with yours. By the time you've circled around to the fourth or fifth back-and-forth, a portrait of your match starts to form in your mind's gallery, detail by vivid detail, no pixels required.

And then, if the fates allow, and the challenges have woven their magic, you'll come face-to-face, not with a stranger, but with someone who's already a chapter or two into the book of you. That's when the avatars bow out, their job done, your match revealed, leaving you to pedal forward on the tandem bike of trust, built sturdy through shared secrets and adventures."

"Why delay the grand reveal?" he asks, still skeptical.

"We're trying to build on more than just looks," I say, hesitating slightly. "I came up with this app because I felt frustrated with how shallow dating seems these days. By focusing on deeper connections from the start, maybe we can find something genuine and lasting."

Mr. Morimoto shakes his head. "It's too unconventional for me. I don't want to invest weeks only to find out my date is a toad."

I resist the urge to tell him that toads aren't even in our avatar lineup. "But what if that toad turned into a princess with just one kiss?" I counter, trying to salvage the conversation.

"Sorry, not interested." He looks at Liv. "Tell your family hello," he says, bowing out—literally—and disconnecting the call.

I stand and slump onto my futon, defeated. "I knew I should've worn those lucky shorts."

Liv moves to the edge, giving my arm a comforting pat. "Don't sweat it. Mr. Morimoto wasn't our knight in shining armor."

"But what if he's onto something? What if the only match for a fire ant is an exterminator?" I ask.

Liv swivels her laptop to face me. "Look, we're a 99% match according to our own algorithm. It works. There's a lid for every pot, a bug for every net."

"I suppose, but it would be better if you had it all ... tall, dark, and handsome with, you know..."

"Oh, I know ... a package deal? Some nice abs, biceps, and, most importantly, rock-solid equipment?"

I nod. "What do we do now?"

"We hope for a miracle," Liv says.

"I thought we'd take the dating world by storm in the same way Elon Musk made space exploration possible."

Liv laughs. "Yes, but with fewer Twitter rants." She squeezes my hand. "Don't give up."

"I won't, but it's hard to keep flitting forward when

the entire world keeps swatting you back," I say, rising to hug my friend. "Your dad wouldn't want to be our financial fairy godfather, would he?"

Liv shakes her head. "No, but he did say I could do whatever I want with my trust fund."

"Really?" My ears perk up.

"Yeah, but there's a catch. I can't touch it until I'm thirty-five."

I slump back into the futon. "Seven years, huh? Do you think my landlord will accept IOUs for that long?"

Liv rises, her eyes alight with a secret. "He might not have to. I've got one last ace up my sleeve. If it works, we won't just be in the game, we'll be the game."

CHAPTER TWO

AJ

Peering down from my office, I marvel at the city stretching out below, a tapestry of life and light. Steel Enterprises stands tall among the skyline, a gleaming beacon of metal and glass, the empire I've built with nothing but brains and ambition.

"Another year, another challenge," I sigh, running a hand through my hair. My team has combed through hundreds of app submissions to find the most promising candidates, and now twenty-five folders clutter my desk, begging for my verdict.

The Great App Challenge has a simple goal: to discover apps that utilize creativity, innovation, and user experience to boost profits.

Only a few contenders show promise, and those are mediocre at best. This year, the apps are lackluster, failing to deliver the innovative and captivating experiences I hoped for. An augmented reality hiking app teases me with pixelated landscapes. A meal planner serves up the same bland recipes. A budget tracker confuses more than it clarifies. Each one a letdown, each one a missed opportunity. Where are the transformative ideas? The apps that could change lives?

Then my gaze falls on a pink-themed folder with a cartoonish ladybug mascot on the front. "Love Bug," the submission reads. An app that uses psychological principles to aid in finding your ideal partner.

I snort. Dating apps are a dime a dozen, and this one is tailored to women. There's profit potential, but I'm not interested in funding another dating app. The last one I used took me to the cleaners with lots of first dates that turned into nothing. With a flick of my wrist, I send the Love Bug proposal into the reject pile. Love Bug is dead on arrival—swatted like a fly.

The rest of the apps aren't much better. As the sun dips below the horizon, a headache throbs at my temples, and my patience frays at the edges. None of these apps are going to be the next big thing. The Great App Challenge will continue—but for now, I'm left with nothing but a waste of time and the bitter flavor of disenchantment, much like the aftereffects of my last relationship.

My fingers knead my temples, trying to massage away the frustration. I remember the dating app that promised unparalleled success but failed to deliver compatible matches. Intrigued by the app's marketing pitch and the buzz surrounding it, I eagerly jumped into the virtual dating world, convinced it would save me time and energy.

But what I encountered was far from the seamless

connection promised. The app's algorithm, designed to prioritize quantity over quality, flooded my inbox with an endless stream of potential matches, each profile more misleading than the last. I sifted through a sea of dubious characters—catfishers, scammers, and individuals with ulterior motives.

I vividly remember one disastrous date that had emerged from this venture. I had agreed to meet a woman who was perfect on paper—beautiful, successful, intelligent, and with similar interests. However, as soon as we sat down for coffee, it became apparent that her focus was on my financial standing.

She barely showed any interest in getting to know me as a person, instead bombarding me with questions about my income, investments, and future financial prospects. It quickly became evident that she saw me as nothing more than a cash cow, a means of upgrading her lifestyle.

Disheartened and disillusioned, I ended the date early, glancing at my pants and excusing myself, telling her I was late to my doctor's appointment to get antibiotics for a nasty infection I got from my last date—my only way to ensure she never contacted me again. But she did, a week later.

It was an eye-opening experience that shattered my remaining faith in dating apps. My bottom line had been under scrutiny, not my character or compatibility. The woman didn't even care if I had a raging case of syphilis, which I did not. The entire experience left me with an aversion to the whole concept.

Steel Enterprises will keep searching for an app that

delivers. And me? I'll stick to what I do best, making money, not love connections.

My cell rings, and I see my mother's smiling face on the screen.

"Hey, Mom."

"AJ, honey, are we still meeting two weeks from next Monday?"

I quickly pull up my calendar and see my mother's name, circled with asterisks marking the time.

"I'll see you at six-thirty."

"The usual place?" she asks.

The usual spot is thirty minutes away, twice that time during rush hour. "Can we meet here? It's the first day of the challenge, and I might be running late. I'll make a reservation at The Pampered Palate. Just you and me, right?" My mother has a habit of interfering in my love life, and by that, I mean she comes up with more eligible women than any app could. I wouldn't put it past her to bring me a harem to choose from. Her need for grandbabies outweighs any respect for my personal space. I sigh, filled with a mix of exasperation and amusement. I understand my mother's good intentions, but her relentless pursuit of finding me a partner often borders on overwhelming. The thought of her orchestrating a potential group of eligible women makes me hyperventilate. My mother, despite everything, is someone I love deeply, and I appreciate her unwavering support.

"See you then, Andrew." She hangs up without answering my question, but I know she's unhappy because she called me Andrew instead of AJ. Only business associates and agitated moms use my birth name.

THE FOLLOWING DAY, I stride into the Steel Enterprises office, coffee in hand, ready to dive into a fresh batch of app proposals. My team has weeded through the remaining applications overnight, and a new stack of finalists awaits me on my desk.

"Good morning, boss," Mary says. "The analysts wanted you to give submission number five another look. They think you might have dismissed it a bit hastily."

I locate the fifth proposal and scowl as I see that familiar ladybug mascot mocking me.

"Love Bug. Again?"

I toss the proposal onto my desk and fix my assistant with a piercing glare. "Tell the analysts we are not resurrecting that ridiculous dating app. We're not peddling pink-themed matchmaking to the masses. Is that clear?"

My assistant gulps but stands firm. "They used their veto, sir. As part of the challenge rules, they get one opportunity to overturn an initial rejection and fast-track the app into the group of finalists. They believe Love Bug has real potential if given a chance."

She scurries out before I can say another word.

"Unbelievable." I snatch up the proposal again, scanning the pages critically. The team proposes a new app layout and streamlining of the features, but at its core,

Love Bug remains the same. It's a frilly piece of nonsense designed to attract starry-eyed romantics.

"No amount of polishing can transform this turd into a diamond." I crumple the proposal into a ball, ready to lob it into the trash. Then I pause.

My analysts are good at their jobs, and I need to remember that. As I reconsider the idea, I can't help but wonder if my skepticism stems from a mix of past betrayals and those dating app disasters that left me cynical about love. Shaking off the memories, I take a deep breath and lay the proposal flat again, viewing the details with cautious optimism.

The more I read, the more I realize this app has potential—not as a matchmaker but as an ingenious social experiment. People love sharing personal details about their dating lives, and if we rigged the questions and matches just so ... maybe it could work as an icebreaker. I'm not convinced it can predict love, but perhaps it can open the door to friendship and lead Steel Enterprises to its next big payday.

I shake my head, chuckling ruefully at the thought of paying money again to outsource my love life to an app. Dating is messy and imperfect, filled with nuance and compromise—things no mobile app could replicate. But according to my mother, it's more of a business transaction. I've seen what a good social match did to my parents. They were virtual strangers until my father died.

My phone buzzes, and I glance at the screen and see a text from Sarah, my head analyst, asking if I finished the other app proposals. *No rest for the wicked.*

I quickly reply, telling her I'd look at them now. My team only has the authority to override one of my decisions per contest, so I choose my rejections carefully. I'll give the app a chance if they feel strongly enough about Love Bug to use their single veto, but I doubt it will win.

For now, though, I have twenty-four other proposals to evaluate. Seeking an app that could produce results, I crack my knuckles and dig into the pile.

The next few hours pass in a blur of buzzwords and unrealistic revenue projections. The lengthening shadows outside my window show how late it has grown when I emerge from my office.

Looking for coffee, I wander into the break room and find my head analyst there. "Don't you have plans tonight?" I ask.

"Not doing anything until we complete the proposals," she replies, shaking her head and stifling a yawn. "I wanted to discuss Love Bug with you if you have a moment."

I frown, but I have promised to consider their input, and it isn't as if I have any better plans.

"Sure," I say. "Convince me." I pour a cup of coffee and doctor it with enough sugar to put a person with diabetes into a coma.

The analyst smiles, no doubt expecting the challenge. I lean against the counter wondering if I'm about to regret giving her the chance.

She takes a sip of her coffee before starting. "You know, Love Bug isn't your run-of-the-mill dating app."

I snort. "It's pink and glittery. What self-respecting man would use it?"

She chuckles. "You'd be surprised. Our research shows men are warming up to apps that are female-centric."

I raise an eyebrow. "Really?"

"Yes," she says, leaning in. "Think about it. If you're looking for a quality steak, you don't go to a hotdog stand, do you?"

"And the avatar system," she continues, "it's not just a gimmick. It actually shifts the focus from looks to shared interests."

I ponder this. "So, it's like a masquerade ball for the digital age?"

She smiles. "Exactly."

I shake my head. "You can't build a real connection without chemistry. How are you supposed to feel that spark with someone when you have no idea what they look like?"

"Chemistry develops in many ways," she counters. "The questions are designed to reveal compatibility on an emotional and intellectual level. And when users reach the level where they can exchange photos, they have already built a foundation of trust and understanding, which leads to a much higher chance of sparks flying in person."

I open my mouth to argue but find I can't deny the logic in her words. I think of my failed relationships, built more on physical attraction than anything of actual substance. If there's even a chance Love Bug could do better, I owe it to myself—and the countless singles navigating the dating scene—to give the app a shot.

"What's this about reaching a level?"

Her smile couldn't have gotten any broader without swallowing her face. "Did I mention that the app has gamification included?"

"No, you did not." This sounds more interesting by the minute. I lean forward. "Tell me more."

The analyst grins, and I shake my head in grudging admiration. My team has always been good at getting what Steel Enterprises wants—profit.

"It takes the matches on adventures designed to remove the participant from their comfort zone. To share things in a personal way that gets at the heart of the matter and the person."

"Well, you had me at gamification and lost me at heart." Gamification means they could install paywalls, which implies that people would have to pay more to move forward with the match, and I like that.

She laughs. "You know, you'll never find love in spreadsheets and bottom lines."

"I'm not looking for love." I kick off the counter and return to my office. In my comfy chair, I steeple my fingers as I mull over the implications of backing an app like Love Bug. On one hand, the dating app market is saturated, and there's no guarantee it would gain enough traction to become profitable. But on the other hand, its unique approach to matching could be the sort of innovation that sets it apart. We will tap into a new demographic and revenue stream if it takes off. I don't have to believe in its ability to make love connections. I need to know if it has the potential to profit.

I pull up the analysts' projections for the app's growth on my computer and study the numbers. According to their research, compatibility-focused dating apps have seen a 30% increase in users over the past year, especially among females. If Love Bug captures even a fraction of that interest, it could bring in a couple of million in revenue within the first year. And if it goes viral … the sky is the limit.

I lean back in my chair with a groan, kneading the tension in my neck. The financials make a compelling case, but I still can't shake my gut response that it's the wrong move. Online dating has left me with nothing but a string of disastrous relationships, and the thought of enabling more of the same leaves an unpleasant taste in my mouth.

Then again, I'm letting my personal biases cloud my judgment. Just because the apps haven't worked for me doesn't mean they can't work for someone else. And at the end of the day, I have a responsibility to my company and shareholders to make the decision that makes the most business sense.

Reluctantly, I accept that it will be a finalist after all. My team has made sure of it. But I don't believe it has what it takes to become the next big thing.

I gather my staff in my office before the end of the workday. "Alright, these are the ten finalists," I say, handing over the list. "Go ahead, send the letters and get them here."

Tanya, my head of product development, breaks into a triumphant grin. "I knew you'd come around. Love Bug has so much potential, Andrew. You'll be thrilled with how it performs."

I raise a warning hand. "Don't get ahead of yourself. Yes, you guys put it in the finals, but that doesn't mean it will win."

She dismisses my concern with a wave of her hand. "The numbers speak for themselves. Love Bug will blow the other apps out of the water."

Despite their enthusiasm, I'm not moved. Their confidence in Love Bug's success seems misguided. "We'll see," I say, choosing not to argue now.

As they leave my office, my team members are buzzing with ideas for refining the apps before the last stage. I sink back into my chair, gaze drifting out the window to the sprawling San Francisco skyline below. The pulse of the city unfolds before me, full of potential, full of possibilities, full of loneliness.

CHAPTER THREE

JUNIE

Bills clutter my kitchen table, a vivid reminder that Love Bug is hemorrhaging funds faster than bandages can staunch the flow. Desperately, my fingers shuffle through the paper mountain again. Perhaps I'll find a winning lottery ticket, or an inheritance notice from a forgotten relative that got lost in the mix. No dice. Staring back are only demands for electric payments, rent, and those relentless web hosting fees.

Frustration mounts as I rake my fingers through my hair, contemplating the financial quagmire I've sunk into. A trio of maxed-out credit cards serves as a testament to my misguided enthusiasm. Countless late nights spent with Liv, fueled by kombucha and Red Bull, dreaming of birthing the next revolutionary dating app. And all for what?

The mail slot groans, spitting out another heap of dread that thumps softly onto the floor. Picking up today's mail, I head back to the kitchen, knowing it's just more of the same.

The sun filters through the window, dappling the chipped Formica countertop with golden light. I squint at the embossed letterhead of one envelope, tracing the swooping calligraphy with a fingertip.

The Great App Challenge.

A jolt surges through my gut. This contest? Never heard of it, let alone entered it.

With trembling fingers, I tear open the envelope and scan the contents. Our dating app, Love Bug, has been selected as one of the ten finalists. Which is strange, considering the app isn't finished yet. I look back at the front and realize it's addressed to Liv but to my address.

Whipping out my phone, I dial Liv's number.

"What's cookin', good lookin'?" Liv's voice is upbeat when she answers.

"Did you enter Love Bug into some kind of contest?" I ask, my voice tinged with disbelief.

"Ah, you found out," she says, a note of hesitation in her voice. "Look, there's a cash prize, a big one. I thought it could be the push we need to finish the app."

I slump onto a stool, staring at the art wall Liv helped me assemble. "You could've consulted me. Was this the 'Hail Mary' you were talking about?"

"I'm sorry," Liv sighs. "I should've talked to you first, but I want this so badly for us, you know? We've been working on Love Bug forever, and I hate seeing you struggle to pay rent and bills. I thought if we won the prize money, it could change everything."

The earnestness in Liv's voice gives me pause. I know she means well, even if her methods are questionable. And she isn't wrong about the money. I'm two months late on my rent and things aren't looking up.

The mere notion of relinquishing our digital offspring to unknown hands sends shivers down my spine. I like being the one in charge. Giving up that control feels utterly alien to me. But perhaps it's time to be more flexible. If I can't trust Liv, who can I trust? We've come this far together. Maybe it's worth giving up control to give Love Bug a fighting chance.

Taking a deep breath, I say, "Just promise me this is the last time you make a decision like this without checking in."

"Absolutely," Liv responds, her voice filled with relief. "Does this mean we're doing the contest?"

A smile tugs at the corner of my mouth. "Apparently, we already are because we're in the finals." I hold my phone away from my ear until she stops screaming. Then we discuss what we must accomplish before she represents us in two weeks.

After I end the call, my mind starts racing. We're contestants in the Great App Challenge. I have so many questions—who are the judges, what's the prize money, how tough is the competition?

A knock at the door interrupts my train of thought. I open it to find a skinny guy in ripped jeans and a Ramones T-shirt holding a stack of yellow papers. He thrusts a page at me. "Eviction notice," he mutters before sauntering away.

I scan the document, my stomach plummeting. Thirty days to pay up or pack up.

Panic surges through me, leaving me breathless. What's my next move? The answer hits me like lightning —we have to win that contest. It's the only way.

Grabbing my phone, I dial Ethan. "We have a problem," I blurt out, skipping the pleasantries. "How are the fixes coming? Please tell me you're ahead of schedule."

"Well, hello to you too," Ethan says, his voice dry. "I'm doing great. Thanks for asking." There's a pause. "Everything is progressing, but we still have some bugs to work out."

"We're out of time," I tell him. "I just got an eviction letter, and we have to be ready for The Great App Challenge."

Ethan inhales sharply. "The Great App Challenge?"

"It's a long story, but Liv entered us, and we're in."

"I've got an app that made the finals too."

"Wait, so you have an app competing with Love Bug?" I ask, my voice edged with disbelief. "How can I trust you to give your all for us?"

He pauses for a second too long. "Honestly? It's a win for me if either app succeeds. But I'm committed to making Love Bug the best it can be."

Inside, I can't help but do the math. If Love Bug triumphs, he takes a 30% cut. But if his app wins, he pockets everything. Yet, with no other options on the table, I realize I have to take that leap of faith. "Alright," I say, trying to sound more confident than I feel. "If you do that, I'll give you a dozen vegan chocolate chip cookies, Liv's favorites." I promise.

Ethan chuckles. "Make them non-vegan, and you'll have the most flawless app the world has ever seen."

"I'm counting on it," I tell him. "Talk to you soon." I hang up, feeling a little lighter thanks to Ethan's confidence, though worry gnaws at me that he might be stretched too thin, considering he also has an app in the competition. We're in for a few late nights, but we can ensure Love Bug takes flight together.

Liv, Ethan, and I throw ourselves into our work with renewed urgency. Fueled by coffee and sheer determination, we pull all-nighters to iron out the bugs in Love Bug and prepare it for the Great App Challenge.

As we dive into our work, the impending eviction presses on my chest like a relentless burden.

Time is ticking, and the stakes couldn't be higher. Losing my apartment means I'm out of options. Mom's out of state, and Liv's cramped studio in Nob Hill barely fits her pull-out sofa, let alone another person. But I set those worries aside for now. Winning this contest is our beacon of hope.

Day by day, Love Bug improves. Ethan codes, Liv designs, and soon, the app is nearly ready. We've polished the interface and tweaked the algorithms. Only the dancing avatars need fixing, but they don't affect how the app works. Now, it's time for Liv to shine in the city.

My phone vibrates with a text from her, just as she's supposed to leave for San Francisco.

I'm sick.

It's unlike Liv to back down, especially since she's always healthy with her clean eating and regular work-outs. I text back.

Get your ass over here. You're going.

Seconds later, my cell rings and an almost inaudible voice croaks from the other end. "I'm seriously sick. It must have been all those all-nighters that wore me down. My doctor says it's mono."

Panic and nausea churn in my stomach. Liv is the face of our team, the social glue that can and will charm the judges. Without her, I'll have to enter the spotlight—an unbearable thought.

"What's our next move?"

"You're gonna do it alone."

My knees buckle, and I reach for the edge of the bed to steady myself.

"Liv, you're the spotlight, I'm the shadow. You have to go."

"I'm contagious," Liv says, and when her coughing fit subsides, she draws in a deep breath and sighs. "We have no choice. It's do or die, Junie. Pull up your knickers and pack your bag."

My hands shake as I say, "We'll have to withdraw from the competition."

"What? No, we can't do that! We've worked too hard. You'll have to present in my place. It's your app. You are more familiar with it than anyone else."

"I can't," I admit, my voice edging into desperation. "You heard me in that call to the investor. I'm a bumbling idiot."

"No, you're not," Liv reassures with a soft smile. "Everyone has off days. Besides, nobody speaks about Love Bug with the fire you do. I believe in you. You've got this."

Her calm confidence only tightens the vise around my chest. I walk into the kitchen for a glass of water, my eyes catching the eviction letter on my fridge—a sober reminder of what's at stake. I feel trapped between the devil and the deep blue sea without a clear direction.

"Leave it to you to get a kissing disease. If it's contagious, then I might have it. See, I can't go."

Liv sighs. "It's called the kissing disease because it's spread by saliva. You and I don't swap spit."

That meant that Liv and someone else did. "Who is he?"

"Late-night pizza guy."

"Seriously?"

"Yes, and it doesn't matter. You are capable of doing this."

"Why do I need to stay there? It's just across the bay."

"Do you have money for daily bus or a taxi rides? No, you don't," she says. "Besides, staying at an all-expenses-paid hotel could be just what you need. Treat it like a vacation."

"You're right. I can handle this." My head screams, "No, you can't," but I silence the naysayer and start packing. "What am I supposed to wear?" My style is more hobo chic than high fashion.

There's a long pause before Liv answers. "Wear

anything but that getup with the stripes and florals or anything else that looks ridiculous."

I can't help but widen my eyes. "So, what you're saying is, don't wear anything in my closet," I say, half-jokingly.

Liv bursts into laughter on the other end of the line. "No, no. I just want you to make a good impression. You know, hobo chic might not be the best look for the Great App Challenge."

I realize that Liv probably has a point. While I embrace my unique style, I also understand that first impressions matter, especially in the competitive tech world.

"Do you still have that blue blazer?" she asks.

"Seriously? You want me to dress like your mother?" Liv's mother had given me the blazer when I showed up at a fundraiser in my signature striped and floral number.

"Yes, it's professional."

"It's boring."

"Boring may get you a hundred grand in winnings."

"Get *us* a hundred grand." I could dress up like a corporate robot if it gets me thirty-three grand—my share of the winnings. That's a lot of rent money. "And yes, I'll stuff my suitcase full of boring, respectable clothes."

Liv laughs, then coughs again. She honestly sounds terrible. "No pairing Vans with anything."

My jaw drops. "They're black and white. They match everything."

"Juniper Parker, if those Vans make an appearance, consider your cookie privileges revoked."

I weigh the threat and finally cave in. "Fine, but that's because those cookies are the bomb, and you pair them with my favorite kombucha." I can't afford the cookies or the kombucha and would miss them. Liv, blessed with an affluent lineage, doesn't juggle the penny-pinching woes that I do. Her regular allowance covers what she needs, essentials stretched to include gourmet bites and tangy brews. Every morsel, every sip she shares, I savor with gratitude.

After a few failed attempts at assembling a Liv-approved outfit, I finally settle on a smart-casual ensemble—well-fitted jeans, a colorful blouse that lets my personality shine, and the dreaded blazer for a touch of professionalism. I pack my Vans and a few favorite tees, just in case.

Looking at myself in the mirror, I can't help but chuckle at the memory of Liv's fashion critique. I know she only has my best interests at heart, and while I appreciate her blunt advice, I also need to stay true to myself.

With my more conservative outfits packed, I finish stuffing my essentials into the bag and take one last look around my apartment. The eviction letter still flaps hauntingly on the fridge, a reminder of the high stakes. But I can't let that dampen my spirits. I have a contest to win and am determined to give it my all.

Clutching my bag, I cross the threshold, my veins buzzing with a cocktail of anticipation and anxiety. The Great App Challenge awaits.

CHAPTER FOUR

AJ

My tie flaps wildly in the San Francisco breeze like a rogue kite as I navigate from Steel Enterprises to the neighboring hotel for dinner with my mother. The clinking glasses and hushed conversations greet me as I enter the bar. It's a high-end place—no flashy neon signs or peanut shells crunching underfoot, just polished mahogany and intimate lighting.

A woman, alone at the bar, draws my attention. Her red hair burns bright in the dim light, a living flame. She's not my typical type, but there's something about her magnetic energy that I can't ignore. I approach the bar, sliding onto the stool next to her. "Mind if I join you?"

She turns to me, a smile gracing her lips. "Um, sure. I'm Junie."

"Name's AJ," I say, taking her outstretched hand. Her grip is solid, a contrast to her surprised expression.

As the bartender sets her drink down, a glass of ice

water, I order a scotch. "So, Junie, what's the occasion? What brings you to San Francisco?"

"I'm here for a passion project," she says, her fingers idly circling her glass. "Thought I'd unwind before heading back to my room."

"Interesting," I say, intrigued. "You rarely hear passion and project in the same sentence these days."

She laughs, and the sound reminds me of wind chimes in a soft breeze. "Well, sometimes you have to follow your heart, right?"

"Right." I raise my glass. "Here's to following your heart." That wouldn't be my mantra, but I understand the sentiment. For me, it's all about following my head—the one on my shoulders.

Our glasses clink, and she sips her water. I'm about to ask more about her project when the door to the bar swings open, and in walks my mother. She isn't alone.

My heart sinks like a stone. The expression on my mother's face and the presence of the woman beside her, Camilla Van Delf, socialite, philanthropist, and serial bride, spell out a familiar, unwelcome scenario. This is one of my mother's setups, and I can't take another one.

On impulse, I turn to Junie. "I know you don't know me, but I need your help. Can you play along?"

She looks startled, her eyebrows furrowing in confu-sion. "Play along with what?"

Before I'm able to explain, my mother descends upon us. "AJ, who's your lovely friend?"

Not missing a beat and hoping the woman at my side joins in, I say, "Mom, this is Junie, my ... girlfriend."

The look on Junie's face is priceless, a fusion of shock and amusement. Her mental gears appear to be in motion. She looks down at her outfit—well-worn jeans, a riotously floral shirt, and a vintage blazer that seems stolen from a 70s TV show wardrobe department. Her look is completed with tennis shoes that clash delightfully with everything she's wearing.

"Girlfriend?" Junie's eyes widen as she turns to me.

"She's the one I can't do without. We haven't put a label on it, but let's just say we're exclusive. So, girlfriend fits." I watch her face shift from disbelief to amusement.

"Absolutely, honey bunch." She turns to Mom with a smile. "I'm Junie, your future daughter-in-law."

That might have been a little over the top, but it works to push my always-in-control mother off kilter. I reach out to steady her when she wobbles on her heels.

My mother, always the polite hostess, recovers quickly, extending her hand with a bemused smile. "Nice to meet you, Junie. I'm Maxine."

While my mom appears shocked, Camilla's expression is priceless. Camilla looks like she's swallowed a wasp. My mom breezily dismisses her with a flick of her wrist. "Camilla, dear, we'll have to take a rain check."

Camilla, utterly stunned, can only nod mutely. Her coiffed blonde curls bobble up and down as my mother points to the door before turning back to face Junie and me.

"Are we ready to eat?"

I stand, offering Junie my arm. She raises an eyebrow at the gesture but takes it. As Mom approaches the restaurant, I lean in, whispering a quiet "thanks" to Junie. She glances at me, a mischievous smirk lighting up her face.

"Don't mention it, AJ," she says, her voice a playful whisper. "Umm ... but just so you know, I'm not a cheap date." She winks, her laughter filling the space between us.

As we stroll behind my mother, I catch her glancing back at Junie's feet, her eyes narrowing on her shoes. "Those shoes," she muses aloud, "are rather interesting."

Junie looks down at her feet and then up at my mother. "Oh, these? I love them. I got my first pair when I was at Folsom Prison."

Mom freezes in her steps, causing me to nearly collide into her. "Prison?" Mom asks.

Junie looks at both of us and must have seen the shock because she blurts out hurriedly, "Not as an inmate! I got my degree in psychology and did an internship there. No one, whether they're prisoners or staff, is allowed laces. Big security risk. But they're kind of a lifesaver for me since I'm ... well, a bit clumsy."

"Really?" Mom asks, her eyebrows raised in amusement. Blushing a little deeper, Junie nods, lifting her canvas-covered foot as evidence. "I've tripped over my laces twice, once breaking my wrist and another time spraining my ankle. So, laces and heels? Not my best friends. When I stumbled upon these sneakers, I grabbed multiple pairs. I've got five in different colors."

Mom gives the sneakers another amused glance. "Just five?"

"Oh, no: I've also bedazzled a pair for fancy dinners out," Junie states proudly.

The laughter that follows is a pleasant surprise. It's refreshing to see my normally prim and proper mother sharing a genuine moment with a stranger, who's turning out to be more interesting by the minute.

At The Pampered Palate, the host leads us into the heart of the restaurant to a cozy spot that exudes a warm candlelit glow, and I realize the act has only just begun. The place is dimly lit, with soft lights bouncing off polished wood and wine glasses. The low hum of conversation melds with the delicate notes of a piano playing in the corner.

Pulling out a chair for Junie, I notice the lift of her brow as if she's not used to this kind of treatment. I give her a playful shrug, as Mom and I take our seats.

"AJ has impeccable manners. Should I thank you for that?" Junie says.

"Yes," Mom says. "Manners are the cornerstone of civility."

We scan the menu, the server appearing not long after. "Decided yet?" he asks, focusing on Junie. She squirms slightly. "Can I get another minute?" He acknowledges with a nod and steps away.

"I think I'll have the vegan lasagna," Junie says.

"Are you a vegetarian?" Mom asks.

"Only when Liv is around. She's a hard-core vegan, and I try to be supportive." She glances around the restaurant. "But ... she's not here tonight, so I can be a full-on carnivore."

Mom stares at me while slightly tilting her head. "Who's Liv?"

I haven't got a clue since I've known Junie for all of twenty minutes. Thankfully, Junie clears her throat, hesitating a moment, as if gathering her thoughts, then comes to the rescue.

"Uh, Liv is ... well, she's my sister from another mister and ... um ... a diehard vegan." Junie leans forward, glancing around as if checking for Liv's presence, her eyes widening for emphasis. "She looks at me like I've just committed murder whenever I order a piece of meat."

I laugh at Junie's dramatics. Her hands fidget with her napkin before they begin to fly as she paints a vivid image of this mysterious Liv and her judgmental glares.

"And, um, let me tell you," Junie continues, a slight blush coloring her cheeks, "I've ... I've spent countless hours studying menus, trying to find something that satisfies my carnivorous cravings and won't send Liv into an existential crisis."

Mom is nearly in stitches, clutching her stomach as she laughs at Junie's antics. "Oh my, so how do you navigate that?"

With a flourish, Junie pulls out the menu again, finger tracing the various dishes listed. "Oh, it's a delicate dance. I start by casually suggesting the pan-seared salmon, and then, when Liv gives me the stink eye, I quickly switch to the quinoa salad. But of course, I want some protein, so I add the grilled chicken, but that's another no-no, so then I ..." Junie trails off... "But of course, tonight, I don't have to worry about Liv's watchful eyes," she concludes, her smile bright and playful.

I flag the waiter over and he once again starts with Junie.

"I'd like to order the New York strip steak, please," she says.

After we place our orders, the server scurries away. Mom turns toward us, her eyes filled with curiosity. "So, how did you two meet?"

Surprised, we both respond simultaneously.

"At a bookstore," Junie says, just as I say, "At the museum."

We look at each other in surprise and then back to my mother, whose brow is arched like she suspects something isn't right. And, of course, she is spot on, but there's no way I'm getting caught.

"Actually, it's a blend of both," I clarify. "I first spotted Junie at the museum, then trailed her to a nearby bookstore."

Mom looks intrigued. "What drew you to each other?"

"We ... um ... reached for the same book," Junie answers, a bit hesitantly.

"Really? What was the title?" my mother asks, her curiosity evident.

"*She Comes First*," Junie mumbles.

Mom's eyes widen, as she almost chokes on her own breath. "That's a ... um ... a very informative read."

Heat creeps up my neck as I meet Junie's eyes. Her hint about picking up a book to improve my ... skills flits through my mind. "Turns out I didn't need it. I'm already well-versed in satisfaction."

Junie's smile widens. "You know what they say? Knowledge is power." She winks at me, and the once-wilting flower of a woman beside me seems to get some strength in her stem as she sits taller.

"And has the book helped?" Mom stares me down.

Caught off guard, I clear my throat. "We're good in that department." I flash a confident smile before turning to Junie. "Right, sweetie?"

Junie's grin spreads across her face. "Absolutely," she says, her voice dripping with faux sincerity. "It's like he's got a map and a compass. Never loses his way."

Mom's eyes widen in surprise. "Well then," she says, raising her water glass in a toast. "To excellent navigation."

Junie excuses herself to use the restroom, and as soon as she's out of sight, Mom says, "She's not what I would have expected."

I knew what my mom expected. She wanted pedigree, and Junie wasn't an Ivy League or fashion week kind of girl. "She's authentically her, and that's a rare find these days."

Mom stared at me for an endless minute before she smiled. "Despite her clear lack of fashion sense, I like her. She's unique. Why didn't you tell me about her?"

"It was a surprise." I recalled our conversation. "It's why I asked if it was only you and me. Now, you can stop trying to set me up."

"Honey, it's what I do."

"Hmmm, no, it's what you try to do. Stop. You can see I'm good."

"What did I miss?" Junie says when she returns.

The server is right behind her with our meals.

"Not dinner," I say.

"AJ, honey, how's work?"

"No talk about work tonight. It's a celebration of love and good food." I dig into my steak and hum, but not nearly as loud as Junie, who seems to replay that scene from *When Harry Met Sally*. I half expect every woman in the place to raise their hand and say, "I'll have what she's having." Hell, I want what she's having.

The rest of the evening zips by. And after dessert, Mom leaves, promising to "Lunch soon, Junie darling."

The tension gradually fades away as we walk out of the restaurant and toward the elevators. I offer Junie my arm, a silent thank you for everything she's done tonight.

Once we reach her room, Junie leans against the door, looking at me with amusement and exhaustion. "I'm sorry about that book thing, AJ. I didn't mean to … well, you know. I'm awkward at best in social situations." She shrugs, her face coloring a touch under the hotel hallway's soft light.

I shake my head. "It's fine, Junie. Trust me. It could've been worse."

"Really? How?" she asks, looking genuinely curious. "I told your mom you needed a manual on how to find a woman's love nub, but in my defense and experience, all men can benefit from reading that book."

"Well, she could've asked for a live demonstration. As

it is, all will be forgotten when we present her with a grandchild." I watch her for a reaction, and I'm not disappointed when her eyes go wide, and a laugh bursts out of her.

As the laughter subsides, I look at her and feel a sense of gratitude. I gently brush a strand of hair away from her face. "Thanks, Junie," I say, kissing her cheek softly. "You were a real sport. I'll never forget this night."

She smiles softly. "Neither will I, AJ. Neither will I."

As I turn to leave, the realization hits me that our paths may never cross again. Yet, I'm happy to have spent time with someone many would label as unusual, but whom I regard as a lifesaver.

CHAPTER FIVE

JUNIE

"What do you mean, you had a date last night? Is the app up and working?"

My shoulders slump, weighed down by the reality that my only match on the app during beta testing was Liv—thanks to our oversight in not setting gender parameters during testing. Liv, on the other hand, gets matched with everyone in the test.

"No, it wasn't an actual date, but I had fun."

"I need some details. You had a date but not a real date?"

I explain my situation with AJ and his mother while I dress. I know I should wear the plain, white, collared shirt under the blue blazer, but the stiff material makes my neck itch. Nerves already fraying, I ditch the itchy, formal shirt for my battle armor—a classic tee proclaiming, "Unstoppable. Powered by Coffee and Curiosity." I pair it with jeans and my red Vans Convicts.

"What are you wearing?"

"Clothes."

"Come on, Junie." Liv coughs. "I'm living vicariously through you."

"Fine, jeans, shirt, blazer, shoes."

"What shirt?"

"You know, a shirt."

"Mmm hmm."

I hesitate, biting my lower lip. "Okay, it's not the professional shirt you would have picked out," I confess with a sigh. "It's my 'Unstoppable. Powered by Coffee and Curiosity' tee. There. Happy now?"

Liv laughs. "Oh, Junie. I should've seen that coming. Classic you."

My fingers toy with the hem of my shirt as I search for the words to articulate my thoughts. "Look, Liv," I begin, "I know you wanted me to be all business-like and fit the part of an entrepreneur. But I've learned that I have to wear what makes me feel powerful, even if it's just a quirky T-shirt. I'm not champagne and caviar. I'm Coke and tacos. And that's exactly who I want to be."

Liv sighs, and I can almost see the smile playing on her lips. "I get it. And honestly? That's why I adore you. You're always unapologetically you. Just ... try not to spill any coffee on that power tee, okay?"

The burden of her disappointment lifts, like a cloud parting to reveal the sun. "I knew you'd understand."

"You need to go, or you'll be late. Knock 'em dead."

"How about only a minor flesh wound? I'd hate to be arrested for homicide on my first high-stakes solo business pitch."

"Alright, fine. Just don't trip over your Vans, okay?" she adds, her laughter echoing over the line.

"No promises." With a deep breath, I hang up and pocket my phone, grab my bag, and head toward the door, ready to take on the world.

The Great App Challenge is taking place in the building next door. I know almost nothing about Steel Enterprises, the man behind it, Andrew Steel, or the challenge. All the research I planned to do last night still sits on my to-do list, thanks to an unexpected detour—AJ.

A smile sneaks onto my lips at the mere thought of him, as if he's a secret I can't help but revel in. His fancy suit fit him like a second skin. Don't get me wrong, I can appreciate a good suit. Something about a man in a tie gets my pulse racing. But guys like AJ? They're out of my league. They're more likely to go for women like Camilla, with her mile-long legs, perfect hair, and flawless makeup. Me? I'm lucky if I can apply mascara without risking an eye injury.

As the elevator doors part, revealing Steel Enterprises, I brace myself for the impending face-off with the man of the hour.

From the photos I pulled up on my way over, I only know his backside—clad in an expensive suit, gazing out over the city through his office's glass walls. His reputation paints him as a ruthless business executive, leading me to expect someone cold, distant, and intimidating.

In contrast, there's AJ. His warmth, charm, and disarming smile made him feel more ... human, approachable, and genuine. Despite our brief and unexpected meeting, he left an indelible mark.

Andrew Steel is a whole different game. This man holds the power to either make or break my future. I'm hoping he has a fraction of AJ's charm and understanding.

Entering the room, I find myself amidst a sea of ten equally jittery app developers.

Among them, I spot Ethan. His gaze meets mine, and he offers a slight nod of recognition.

"Everyone, please help yourselves to coffee and donuts." A friendly assistant named Ms. Clark gestures toward a table laden with an array of donuts and a gigantic coffee carafe. "Mr. Steel will be with you shortly."

Grateful for the distraction, I gravitate toward the table and grab a donut smothered in rainbow sprinkles. I return to Ethan, donut in one hand, coffee in the other.

"Hey, Ethan," I greet, attempting to balance my nerves with casual banter.

"Hey, Junie," he replies, eyeing the donut in my hand. "I thought Liv was coming."

"She's got mono."

Ethan steps back. "That's contagious."

"I haven't been kissing her."

The sudden hush that falls over the room cuts our exchange short. I look up as the door swings open and a tall man strides in. My breath catches. I freeze. Because standing there, in all his suited glory, is AJ.

In my shock, my grip slackens around my coffee cup,

and before I can stop it, hot coffee spills all over the front of my "Unstoppable" shirt.

A yelp escapes my lips, loud enough to echo down to the streets below.

"Are you alright, Miss...?" AJ's voice is cool and reserved, starkly contrasting to the warm tones I remember last night.

"Parker. Junie Parker," I mumble, my hands ineffectively patting my coffee-soaked shirt. "I'm okay. It's hot."

His gaze narrows slightly, and something in his expression hardens. He waves his assistant over. "Ms. Clarke, please assist Miss Parker in cleaning up." His eyes never leave mine. "And perhaps find her a dry shirt to change into. We can't have her pitching in a coffee-stained tee."

The assistant nods, rushing over to my side. As I'm led away, I glance back over my shoulder at AJ—no, Andrew Steel, because I don't know this man, and he acts as if he doesn't know me.

As they usher me out, our eyes lock, his filled with a mysterious look that leaves me puzzled. There's a cool distance in them as if his mother wasn't the only one duped the night before.

I return from my room thirty minutes later, wearing the dreaded white blouse I'd dismissed earlier that morning but packed just in case. Somehow, it feels even itchier now than it did then. I quietly slip back into the room, trying not to draw any more attention to myself. It's a futile endeavor.

At the head of the room, Andrew Steel—the epitome

of a formidable businessman—stands tall, every word he utters commanding the room's full attention. His eyes sweep the room, landing on me, filled with steely professionalism.

"Everyone here stands on equal footing," he begins, his deep voice resonating in the silent room. "You'll each have complete access to my team this week. I encourage you to make the most of their vast experience and extensive knowledge."

He paces the room, his voice resonating with the anticipation of what's to come. "In addition, we will assign you a marketing director. They will help you tailor your product to reach the widest potential audience. At the end of the challenge, the app that generates the most profit will be the victor."

As his gaze sweeps over me again, he adds, "Success in this competition is not about who you know but what you bring to the table. It's about innovation, creativity, and the willingness to take risks."

The room erupts into murmurs as he steps down, but before he exits, he stops beside me. "Meet me at the bar at six," he murmurs, his eyes never meeting mine. "We have some things to discuss."

And just like that, he's gone, leaving me to wonder what in the hell I've gotten myself into.

The remainder of the day flies by, consumed by a barrage of meetings. Staying in the adjacent hotel now makes perfect sense. There would be no time to commute with all that needs to get done. Steel Enterprises doesn't do things in halves. Marketing teams, developers, user experience experts—I meet so many people that the names and faces blur together. Through it all, the clock on the wall seems to tick louder as the appointed hour of six approaches.

Finally free from the clutches of the final meeting, I collapse into a nearby chair and fish out my phone. I dial Liv's number, and she picks up on the second ring.

"Hey, Junie," she greets. "How was your first day?"

"Hey, Liv, oh my gosh, you'll never guess what happened." I blurt out in a whisper, my words tumbling over each other in my rush to tell her everything.

"Wait, wait, slow down. What's with all the noise? Where are you?"

"I'm at the challenge, Liv, and you won't believe..."

"Hold on," she interrupts. "Start from the beginning."

"Okay, so you remember AJ from last night, right? The guy I pretended to be on a date with to save him from his mom and her matrimonial plans? So, get this—he's not just AJ, Liv. He's Andrew Steel. Yes, that Andrew Steel. The guy I'm supposed to be convincing to invest in our app. I only find this out when I see him walk into the room this morning during the challenge, and then I spill my coffee all over my 'Unstoppable' shirt, and everyone's staring, and now I have to go meet him at six, and Liv, I don't know what to do!"

There's a long silence on the other end. "Okay, first, breathe. Second, did you say Andrew Steel as in *the* Andrew Steel? And third, why are you always in these crazy situations?"

"Why, thank you, Liv. Always so supportive," I reply, sarcasm dripping from my words.

"Here's what you need to do. First, keep it professional. Don't let what happened last night influence your actions today. Second, focus on your pitch. This is a great opportunity for you—for us. Don't let this mix-up ruin it."

"The problem, Liv," I cut in, "is this isn't one of those pitch meetings. This feels like I'm walking to the guillotine, like Marie Antoinette. Except I didn't even get to eat cake first, and let's be real, cake would've been a nice last meal."

There's a brief pause, and I hear Liv's laughter ringing through the phone. "Okay, Junie, you have a way of painting a picture. But seriously, listen to me. There's no way you could be in trouble, not really. You didn't know AJ was Andrew Steel, did you?"

"No, I didn't," I admit. "But what if AJ thinks I did?"

"Then you tell him the truth. It's as simple as that."

"The truth," I repeat, mulling over the words. "You know, Liv, 60% of people lie at least once during a ten-minute conversation. He might think I'm part of that 60% and won't believe me."

"Then you let your truth stand," she says firmly. "You didn't know, and that's a fact. If he chooses not to believe you, that's on him, not you. Now go on, off with your head. Or not. Preferably not."

CHAPTER SIX

AJ

A quiet satisfaction comes with owning the room, a power that's both intoxicating and treacherous. As Andrew Steel, I wield it daily, letting it run through my veins like a potent drug. But today, as I wait at the bar, swirling the amber liquid in my glass, that power feels oddly tenuous.

The screech of rubber soles against polished wood snaps me to attention. I turn slightly, taking in her figure as she walks over, a careful balance of determination and trepidation evident in each step.

"Junie," I say, my voice a calibrated blend of ice and fire.

"Mr. Steel," she replies, hesitating slightly before using my name. Her eyes are trained on mine, searching for ... something.

"Sit." I gesture to the barstool beside me, taking another sip of my whiskey.

She does, her posture straight, hands folded neatly on the bar. "You wanted to see me?"

I could dance around the topic, but that's not me, so I cut to the chase. "If you think last night's charade gives you any advantage, you're mistaken."

Her head recoils, as though my words were a physical blow. "I'm not the one who started the conversation or the ruse. I didn't know who you were. You approached me and shanghaied me into your charade."

My eyes bore into her, skepticism, and curiosity waging war within me. "You're telling me you didn't know who I was when we had dinner? You didn't look me up when you got the invite?"

"That's what I'm saying." She grimaces. "That's not exactly true."

"I thought not."

She holds up a hand and says, "Wait a minute and let me finish." She pulls her phone from her back pocket and scrolls for a second. "On the way to the hotel, I pulled this up." She turns the phone to show a picture of me looking out the window. "I didn't apply for the competition. Liv was supposed to be here, not me. She's the one who does the pitches, the meetings, all of it. But she got sick ... she got mono."

I raise an eyebrow. Not at the mention of Liv or the illness but at the urgency in Junie's voice. It's raw, defensive, and oddly captivating. I'm no stranger to people trying to get close to me for my wealth and influence. Could Junie be one of them?

"Why didn't Liv inform the committee of her absence?" I ask.

Junie shifts uncomfortably. "She did, but it was last minute."

I nod, taking another sip. There's silence, a period where neither of us speaks. In that quiet, I'm reminded of last night, of how she laughed so freely, her eyes twinkling with mischief—a stark contrast to the tense woman sitting next to me now.

"You really didn't know?" I ask, finally breaking the silence.

She turns to me, her gaze unwavering. "Why would I lie? What would I gain? The competition is about talent and innovation, not about whom I know or pretend to know. If I wanted to gain an unfair advantage, it wouldn't be by pretending to date someone I had just met."

She's tossing my words back at me.

The bartender arrives and asks if she'd like a drink. Junie nods and tells the bartender she'd like that drink with the Amaretto, Vodka, Irish Cream and Galliano. "One screaming orgasm, coming up." The red rising from her neck bleeds color into her cheeks.

"Seriously, that's what it's called?" I ask.

"Don't knock it until you try it." Seconds later, a creamy concoction with whipped cream and a cherry is set before Junie.

"That looks like dessert."

"It's a good way to end the day."

I think about its name and chuckle. "The drink or the

orgasm?" I know I shouldn't have said that. It's wrong in all ways, but I couldn't help myself.

"Why choose one when you can have both?"

I raise my glass. "I'll drink to that."

"Now that you know I'm not out to dupe you, can I go?"

"Before you leave, I want to make something clear," I begin, leaning in slightly so our faces are inches apart. The intimate proximity is deliberate, to see if the once-timid Junie is growing a backbone. "What happened between us yesterday will not influence this competition. If you're expecting special treatment because of our ... unconventional meeting, you're mistaken."

Indignation ignites in Junie's eyes, a firestorm in an emerald sky. "I wouldn't dream of it. I'm here to win on my own merits."

"Good," I say simply. "Then we understand each other."

"We do," she replies, though her voice wavers slightly. "From this point on, we don't know each other."

It's a bold statement, one I didn't expect. I watch her momentarily, surprised at the steel in her voice. But I agree with a nod.

There's a moment, suspended in time, where our eyes lock, and a thousand unsaid words seem to pass between us. Then, just as suddenly, it's gone.

"Isn't this cozy?" a voice from behind us says. I turn to see Ethan and several of the other competitors.

"Not cozy in the least." Junie smiles, her earlier fire now replaced by unwavering professionalism. "If there's nothing else, I should go. There's a lot to prepare for." She turns to Ethan. "Mr. Steel is buying the first round." She lifts her glass so the rest can see she's already been served. "I'd try the Johnny Walker Blue Label. I hear it's the best, and according to Mr. Steel, he's not one to compromise."

The contestants crowd the bar and order the most expensive drinks available. Junie walks away, but I remain there, my thoughts swirling. I thought I had Junie figured out, but our conversation tonight made me realize there's more to her than meets the eye.

After settling the bill, I retreat to the sanctuary of my office. The mahogany desk, the high-back chair, and the familiar scent of leather-bound books provide a welcome comfort.

It's not a matter of distrust, but of needing irrefutable proof of Junie's honesty, so I pull the file. I see that Olivia Kato was on the original application, and a note about her illness and replacement is paper clipped to the front. Junie was telling the truth.

As I settle into my thoughts, my phone's sharp trill breaks the silence. Recognizing my mother's custom ring-tone, I take a deep breath before answering.

"Hello, Mother."

"AJ." Her voice is a mix of excitement and authority. "I've got two extra tickets to the charity gala for the Museum of Fine Arts in two weeks. I expect you to be there. And bring Junie."

Stifling my surprise, I attempt to interject, "Mom, Junie and I aren't—"

"Together?" My mother laughs. "Oh, honey, that was obvious. She's not even your type. And the poor girl doesn't have any fashion sense. Did you see those shoes? And to think she has them in five different colors."

"Don't forget about the bedazzled pair."

"Can you imagine?"

A strange urge to champion Junie surges within me. But more importantly, I hate that my mother sees right through me. If I confess to it all being a ruse, I'll be matched up with Camilla again because my mother refuses to take no for an answer. There's no way that's going to happen.

"Mom, Junie and I are together. She's exactly my type—authentic, unfiltered."

"Then I'll see you both at the gala." Mom hangs up, and I sit there and sigh heavily, staring at the illuminated skyline outside my window. The conversation with Junie replays in my mind—from now on, we don't know each other. How can I ask her to be my date again? The answer is painfully clear. I shouldn't, but I have to. My thoughts drift to the hefty bar tab she left in her wake. She owes me.

CHAPTER SEVEN

JUNIE

My feet carve anxious circles into the hotel carpet as Liv's voice crackles through the phone. She's always been the better half of our team, the one who can actually talk to people without stumbling over words. Here I am, about to go into a meeting about the appeal of our app with the man who knows me as a bedazzled shoe lover.

"Junie, you've got this," Liv reassures me, her voice confident and calming. "Just keep your cool. Focus on what you're there for and keep it professional. You don't know him, remember?"

I grimace at the irony of the situation. AJ Steel. Powerful, confident, and utterly exasperating. He's just as much an enigma to me as I must be to him. Two days ago, he was my fake boyfriend, and now we have to pretend we're strangers.

"I don't know him," I say, as if saying it aloud might cement it in my brain. "Except for dinner and that one screaming orgasm."

A beat of silence follows, and then Liv bursts into laughter. "Please tell me you mean the drink."

I roll my eyes, thankful she can't see my blush. "Of course, I mean the drink. And I'll never order it again. But seriously, it's like he already hates me."

"How can he hate you? No one hates you." She pauses for a moment. "Okay, maybe Martina does, but you knocked over the champagne fountain at her wedding, which knocked over the cake, hit the head table, and knocked over the candle, starting the venue on fire."

"In my defense, I told her I couldn't wear those shoes. They were five inches tall." Martina was a college acquaintance and, come to think of it, I hadn't heard from her since her wedding.

"Just stick to the script, talk about the app, and ignore any personal jab he might throw your way. You're there to represent the app, nothing else. You got this."

"Thanks, Liv. I wish you were here."

"I know, me too. But you're amazing. You can handle this."

"How are you feeling?"

"Like I could sleep until next year."

"Get some rest. I'll do my best to make you proud."

"I'm already proud."

With her encouragement ringing in my ears, I hang up the phone and prepare to head to the meeting room. Today is day two of five. This week is about fine-tuning the launch before they send us home to wait, watch, and pray.

As I enter the meeting room, my stomach twists into a

knot. Andrew Steel is at the head of the table, surrounded by competitors and staff members. Today, he's wearing a tailored charcoal-gray suit, each seam and stitch tailored to perfection. The sharp lines of the jacket accentuate his broad shoulders, and the crisp white shirt beneath adds a touch of elegance to his imposing figure. His tie is a muted shade of blue, understated yet distinctive.

During dinner with his mother, I saw a different side of him that was open and vulnerable. The memory of that evening is in stark contrast to the man I see before me now. Where before there was a spark of warmth, now I only see a business executive's calm, calculated demeanor.

I yearn for that other side of him, the one who laughed at his mother's fashion critique and teased me over drinks. I wonder if that version of Andrew Steel was just a fleeting illusion or if it's hidden beneath the grumpiness, waiting to be uncovered.

His handsome features are both a magnet and a mystery. The ruggedness of his jaw, the intensity of his eyes, the way his suit hugs his form—it's all part of a carefully-constructed image. But what lies beneath? What drives the man who can effortlessly switch between a delightful dinner companion and a relentless investor?

As I sit, I force myself to focus on the task. Thoughts of that night, of AJ's warmth, have no place here. But as the meeting begins, and his resonant voice fills the room, I can't shake the feeling that the Andrew Steel I met at dinner is still hidden behind the mask.

It's a tantalizing thought, one that adds a layer of difficulty to an already challenging situation. I'm here for a purpose—to win this competition and to secure the future of our dating app. But I can't ignore the curiosity that nags at me, the desire to strip the suit from the man— metaphorically, of course.

I shake my head, a silent reprimand for my wandering thoughts. The Andrew Steel I need to focus on is the one before me now, the formidable entrepreneur, not the man who might smile when no one's looking.

I take my seat, carefully arranging my face into an expression of calm professionalism. No recognition, no acknowledgment. Per our agreement, we are now strangers.

AJ's eyes flick to me as I settle in. His gaze is inscrutable, but something in his eyes suggests he's playing the game, too.

He opens the meeting with a few general remarks, outlining the purpose of the discussion and the importance of the apps' appeal to different demographics. Then he turns to me, and his tone changes.

"Miss Parker," he begins, his voice dripping with a mix of curiosity and challenge, "I must ask, why bugs? Of all the things to personify, why not something that might make people feel better about themselves? Wouldn't a woman want to be represented as something more graceful, like a gazelle, and a man more powerful, like a lion?"

Attempting to stand and assert my authority, I misjudge the proximity of the chair's leg, stumbling slightly. A brief gasp ripples through the room, and heat flushes my cheeks. AJ raises an eyebrow, a hint of amusement in his eyes. I try to recover gracefully but all I want is to run back to my room and climb under the covers. This was Liv's job and I'm making a mess of it. Then I hear her voice, *You've got this,* so I press on.

"Clearly, I'm more graceful in the digital world than in the physical one," I say, eliciting a few chuckles from the room. The tension dissipates a little, as I grasp at the lifeline of humor. Gathering myself, I dive in. "Our app, Love Bug, isn't just another dating gimmick. It's about recognizing and celebrating the quirks that make us uniquely human. Much like bugs with their diverse behaviors and looks, humans, too, are an intricate blend of personalities. Through our app, users discover a bug that reflects their true nature, offering a playful yet insightful self-reflection.

"Love Bug isn't about appealing to stereotypes or superficial desires," I say, my voice steadier than I feel. "It's about embracing the uniqueness that makes us human. As bugs have diverse and intricate behaviors and appearances, so do people. By connecting with a bug that mirrors their personality, users find a fun and unexpected way to reflect on who they are."

AJ's eyebrows rise slightly. "But is that what people really want?" he presses. "Don't people usually strive to be viewed as something more glamorous or heroic?"

"People strive to be understood, to be seen," I reply, leaning forward slightly, my passion for our app and confidence bubbling up. "Our app offers a fresh and creative perspective on self-discovery. It's not about wearing a mask or pretending to be something you're not. It's about finding joy in who you really are."

The room is silent for a moment as my words sink in. His eyes lock onto mine.

"And you think an avatar of a bug will keep someone interested? Most people want to see what they're getting," he continues, his voice dripping with skepticism.

I feel a spark of irritation but also a thrilling sense of challenge. He might be a formidable man, but today, I will not be intimidated. Not here, not now. And especially not after the glimpse of the real man I thought I saw the other night.

I step forward, my voice calm but firm. "Mr. Steel, think of it like a box of Cracker Jacks. If you dig straight to the bottom for the prize, you miss the best stuff, like the caramel-coated popcorn and peanuts. Our app is more than just a superficial experience. It encourages users to explore and engage with the content, not just rush to an end result. We challenge the user by having them discover places and things that they might have otherwise skipped. There's a reason we don't show you a person's picture until you've completed several of these challenges. It helps you get to know your match better and undoubtedly learn something about yourself."

A ripple of interest spreads through the room, and I see competitors and staff members nodding in agreement.

Andrew Steel's eyes narrow slightly, and for a brief second, I think I see a flash of amusement. "A noble idea, but people are impatient. They want results, not a journey. A lion, a tiger, a gazelle—these avatars resonate with strength and grace. A bug? It's hardly inspiring."

I raise an eyebrow, my voice taking on a teasing note. "Well, Mr. Steel, not everything that glitters is gold. Sometimes, the things that don't immediately catch your eye prove to be the most rewarding. You know, like finding a diamond in the rough or enjoying the nuances of a fine wine. Our bug avatar represents growth, transformation, and potential. It's not just about what you see, it's about what you can become."

Andrew Steel's lips twitch, and for a fleeting moment, I think I see the trace of a smile. But then it's gone, replaced by his usual stern expression. "We'll see if your philosophy resonates with the market, Miss Parker."

His tone might be dismissive, but I can't help but feel a thrill of victory. I've made my point, held my ground, and maybe, just maybe, I've cracked his frigid exterior briefly.

"Yes, Mr. Steel, we will," I reply, sitting back in my chair, satisfied that I've had the last word. Pride blooms within me—a warm flush of triumph.

The meeting continues with more questions and discussions about the different apps. By the time the gathering concludes, I'm filled with a strange mix of victory and uncertainty. I've presented our app well and didn't let AJ's probing questions throw me off balance.

But something else, something that lingers in the air between us. A connection that goes beyond business, beyond the competition.

I can't help but glance at him one more time. Our eyes meet, and for a brief, electric moment, the façade drops, and we see each other for what we are. And then the moment is gone. The masks are back up. I gather my things and head for the door. My mind is whirling with everything that's been said, every glance exchanged, and the undercurrent of tension that seems to vibrate between us.

As I stride toward the elevator, each squeak of my tennis shoes is a comforting reminder of my individuality. I press the button, and the doors slide open, welcoming me into the empty car. I step inside, feeling a strange release as the doors close.

But then, just as I'm about to escape, a hand snakes through the narrowing gap, stopping the doors from closing. My heart jumps into my throat as AJ Steel strides into the elevator, his eyes locking onto mine.

"You owe me, Junie," he says, each syllable a leash on his emotions.

Laughter escapes me, my nerves making the sound slightly hysterical. "Owe you? For what?"

"The top-shelf drinks you volunteered me to buy last night. That bill was quite hefty."

My laughter dies, and I look at him, stunned. "You can't be serious. I can't even afford rent. I'm certainly not reimbursing you for the alcohol."

He leans back against the wall, a smirk playing on his lips. "I said nothing about money. You can pay me back by attending a gala with me."

I blink, taken aback by his proposal. The memory of

our previous "date" flashes through my mind, and a mix of anticipation and dread swirls in my stomach.

"A gala?" I repeat, trying to keep my voice steady. "Why would you want me there?"

He shrugs, his eyes never leaving mine. "It's you or Camilla, and you know how I feel about that. Besides, you owe me. So, what do you say?"

I study him for a moment, and despite my reservations, despite everything, I nod.

"Alright, Mr. Steel. I'll go to the gala with you."

His eyes flicker with something I can't quite read, and then the doors open, and we step out into the hallway, our deal sealed.

Before I can turn away, I ask, "What does one wear to a gala?"

He laughs at my jeans and "Mind Games Specialist" T-shirt. "Not that. Do you have an evening gown?"

"Sure, it's made of flannel and has cute little bears on it. Maybe you should go with Camilla. I'm sure her closet is full of formal wear," I say, crossing my arms defensively.

He lifts a brow, his expression turning serious. "You're the one who told my mother you were her future daughter-in-law."

I burst into laughter, surprised he was bringing up that playful comment. "You can't be serious. There's no way she believed me!"

His eyes narrow, and he shakes his head slowly. "No, she didn't. But my mother is like a dog with a bone regarding something she wants. And right now, she wants me to marry someone suitable, someone like Camilla."

A strange flutter dances in my stomach when I realize he's serious. "So, you want me to ... pretend? At the gala?"

"Yes," he says firmly. "And you'll have to be more convincing this time. If there's one thing I'm not doing, it's marrying Camilla."

"Why not? She seems more your type," I reply.

"My type? What type would that be?" he asks, raising an eyebrow.

"Oh, you know," I wave a hand dismissively, "polished, posh, perfect hair, perfect nails, perfect everything. The kind who wouldn't be caught dead in this getup." I point to my outfit.

He chuckles, leaning against the wall. "And you think that's what I want?"

"Isn't it?" I challenge.

He shakes his head, a slow smile spreading across his face. "Junie, you'd be surprised at what I want. Perfect is boring. I need someone who can challenge me and keep me on my toes. Someone who wants more than just the Cracker Jack prize. I want someone who loves the peanuts and caramel popcorn."

His words echo in my head, repeating what I'd said earlier that day. It's like he's peeled back a layer of himself, letting me see something real and raw. My heart skips a beat, and I find myself caught in his gaze, unable to look away.

"You don't really mean that," I finally say, my voice

softer than intended, betraying the strange emotion inside me.

"Oh, but I do," he whispers, his eyes still locked on mine.

I swallow hard, my throat suddenly dry. What was happening here? This is AJ Steel, the hard-nosed financier known for his ruthless tactics and frosty demeanor. And yet, here he is, talking to me about peanuts and caramel popcorn like it's the most natural thing in the world.

"I don't know what you want from me, AJ," I say, my voice quivering.

He reaches out, gently tucking a stray strand of hair behind my ear. His touch is warm and tender and sends a shiver down my spine.

"I just want you to go to the gala." The sincerity in his voice and the softness in his eyes all leave me breathless. For a moment, I let myself believe him. Maybe, just maybe, something is happening between us. "You're someone who won't want anything from me but what I'm offering."

"What are you offering?"

He steps back. "A dress for the gala and a way for you to pay me back."

And all the warm fuzzies leave. This isn't about anything but the bar bill and his mother. "One night, AJ, and then you're on your own."

He nods, still smiling. "Deal."

"But one thing you should know, one night with me is

worth a thousand with anyone else." The words slip out, unbidden, but they empower me.

"Something tells me you'll make it memorable." As he walks away, I'm left with a strange sensation of anticipation and uncertainty.

"Let's pray there aren't any open flames," I say under my breath.

CHAPTER EIGHT

AJ

The week was an emotional rollercoaster. I mostly stayed away from Junie, except when I couldn't help but look her way.

The conflicting feelings were too much, and I needed space to breathe—to think. So, instead of handling the competition myself, I handed over the reins to Henry, my best friend, and the CFO of Steel Enterprises, and stayed in my office as much as possible.

On Friday, he steps into my office, closing the door behind him.

"All the apps are live." He sits across from me, and leans back, studying me for far longer than I'm comfortable with.

"Great, thanks for taking over." I stare down at the projections.

"What's going on, man?" Henry asks, sounding puzzled.

"What do you mean?"

"I'm trying to figure out what's going on with you and the Love Bug girl?" he asks, his tone teasing.

I shake my head. "Nothing. She's just another competitor."

Henry coughs into his hand, but the word "bullshit" is loud and clear. "Come on. You can't fool me. I've seen how you look at her when you think no one's watching. The way you pause when she's talking like you're hanging on every word."

A flush creeps up my neck, burning all the way to my ears. "That's absurd."

"It's not," he insists. "Look, I've known you for years. You don't react to people like this unless they mean something to you. And Junie, well, she seems to have gotten under your skin."

I lean back in my chair, frustration mounting. "She's part of the competition, nothing more." There's no way I'm going to let Henry know anything about how I'm feeling about Junie. Mostly, it's because I don't understand it myself. She's not my type. She's unconventional, witty, and doesn't hesitate to challenge me. Where I'm used to order, control, and sophistication, she brings chaos, humor, and a complete disregard for how things are done. I'm torn between admiring her and being annoyed by her.

And those damn tennis shoes and graphic T-shirts she wears? It's as if she's purposefully trying to get under my skin.

I can't stop thinking about the shirt she wore today. It's not just any shirt. It's a defiant declaration. "I Aim to Misbehave." It's printed in bold, in-your-face letters across her chest.

I can't help but picture her wearing it this morning, a twinkle in her eye, knowing the reaction it would provoke. That shirt is so ... Junie. Rebellious, unapologetic, and completely unafraid to challenge convention.

"What's eating you?" Henry asks, catching my far-off stare.

"That shirt Junie wore today," I say, shaking my head. "Did you see it?"

He chuckles. "The 'I Aim to Misbehave' one? Yeah, I saw it."

"Do you think it's a message?"

Henry laughs. "They say well-behaved women rarely make history. We're after history-making, and if that shirt gives her the courage to step outside the norm and do something incredible, I'm all for it."

I have to admit, he's right. And the shirt is unmistakably her. It's like a banner for her personality—daring, unconventional, and always willing to push the envelope.

"She's not really my type," I say to Henry, sounding more serious than I mean to. "But there's something about her that's undeniably appealing."

He raises an eyebrow, a knowing smile playing on his lips. "Sounds like someone's more intrigued by the misbehaving psychologist than he's willing to admit." He smiles. "Everyone loves a bad girl."

"But that's the issue. She's not a bad girl. She's just pretending. I've been watching her—"

"Told you."

I wave him off but can't shake the feeling that he might be onto something. And the truth is, I don't know. All I know is that Junie is nothing like the women I usually date. She's not polished or restrained and certainly doesn't fit into the world I've built around myself. But that's precisely what makes her so intriguing, so different. She's refreshingly genuine and unpredictable, and I am drawn to her, and I hate that I am.

"She's nothing but a potential paycheck." I rub my temples, pushing the thought away. No, Junie and I are incompatible, and I must remember that. The competition is all that matters right now. Today, she leaves to return home, and we're done except for the gala. Once she's out of sight, she'll be out of mind.

Henry's eyes narrow as he studies me, his expression thoughtful. "If you say so. But I've watched you. There's something there." He pauses, letting his words sink in. "You're guarded, and I understand why. Sophia did a number on you." Henry's voice softens with a hint of sympathy.

A pang of unease surges within me. The mere mention of Sophia's name brings back a flood of memories, of vulnerability, of betrayal. My chest tightens, recalling the sting of her deceit. Could one person's actions truly ruin me for all other relationships? I'm unwilling to entertain the idea.

"She's not Sophia," Henry says, breaking through my internal turmoil.

I meet his gaze, defenses up. "I don't want to talk about it."

Henry leans back, raising his hands in mock surrender. "Fine. Let's talk about the challenge itself. I'll bet you that Love Bug wins. It's got heart, something different." The change in topic provides a welcome relief, but the shadow of Sophia's betrayal lingers, a ghost I've yet to exorcise.

"I'll take that bet," I respond, glad for the change of topic. "But I think Stridemaster has a stronger chance. I'm putting my money on it."

He grins. "Okay, I guess it's time to up the stakes. What's the bet this year?" Henry asks, leaning forward. "I still can't believe you made me sing karaoke at the company party."

"You lost, and that was the deal." I'll never forget Henry's off-key rendition of "Sweet Caroline."

He laughs, then grows serious. "Alright, if you lose, you deliver lunch to the entire building dressed as the Love Bug mascot. Imagine it, AJ, you in bright red and black ladybug tights, complete with wings, antennae, and a little tutu."

I grimace, imagining myself in such an outfit. The embarrassment would be unbearable. "If you don't win, you have to run the San Francisco marathon."

Henry rubs his chin thoughtfully. "I can do that."

I raise an eyebrow. "You, Henry? You're more likely to run to the fridge than in a race."

He scowls playfully. "Hey, I can do it. But I won't lose. Love Bug is innovative. It's an app that connects people romantically and helps them understand each other on a basic human level. It's the future of online dating. And it's going to win."

I lean back in my chair, considering everything. "Alright, it's a deal. Stridemaster's unique approach, connecting runners around the globe and turning fitness into a communal experience, will take the prize. And I can't wait to see you huffing and puffing through those 26 miles."

Henry extends his hand, and we shake on it, making it official.

"But be warned," he says, a slow smile spreading across his face, "I have already found a perfect ladybug costume for you. It's waiting, just in case, and I'll capture every moment."

I groan but then start to chuckle. The bet is ridiculous, but it's a part of our friendship tradition. In some strange way, it makes the competition even more exciting.

Henry is gathering his things to leave when a knock comes at the door.

"I guess that's my cue," he says. "Catch you later."

I raise my hand in a half-hearted salute as he heads to the door. But when he opens it, Junie stands on the other side, her eyebrows raised in surprise.

"Oh, hey, Henry," she says, stepping back to make room for him to leave.

Henry grins at her, then turns back to give me a

knowing look. "I was just on my way out. AJ, Junie." With that, he exits, leaving the door slightly ajar.

Junie turns to me, her face open and earnest. "Can I have a moment of your time?" she asks.

"Of course," I say, gesturing to the chair across from me. "What's on your mind?"

Junie comes in and sits where Henry was. "So, I was thinking about the gala next weekend," she begins, her eyes flicking away as if uncertain how to proceed. "You've been avoiding me all week, so maybe you've changed your mind about taking me."

"No, I haven't changed my mind," I say, leaning forward. "I've just been ... busy."

"Busy," she repeats, her voice flat.

"Yes, busy." I force a smile, trying to lighten the mood. "But I promised you a shopping trip, didn't I? Are you a local, or do I need to arrange a flight?" Somehow, the detail of her location slipped past me. Ever since she burst into my scene, my thoughts have been all over the place.

"I live across the bay."

Relief washes over me. "Why don't I pick you up on Sunday at your place?"

Her face lights up, and she scribbles her address and number on a piece of paper for me. "It's a date." Her cheeks were pink. "I don't mean an actual date. I mean, you know, a fake date because I owe you."

I choke on a laugh. "I knew what you meant." I rub my chin. "Do you date a lot?"

She shrugs, her eyes looking everywhere but at me. "Not really. My personality isn't exactly everyone's cup of tea. Being unique can be lonely. That's why I designed the Love Bug app. For people like me who are looking for something more."

"And have you found the 'more' you're looking for from an app?"

She laughs. "All I get are guys in graphic tees. It's like a never-ending parade of slogans."

"Seems like a match made in heaven," I say, glancing at her shirt.

"Sadly, the shirts have been the best part of the dates." She stands, extending her hand to me. "See you Sunday."

"See you Sunday," I repeat, shaking her hand and watching her walk out the door.

She stops and turns around. "I know you're not a believer in dating apps, or maybe you don't believe in love." She hesitates, her eyes meeting mine. "But who knows?" She gives me a challenging look. "You should give Love Bug a try, too. Maybe you'll find what you didn't know you were looking for." She closes the door behind her.

I lean back, holding the paper tightly, a slow smile forming on my face. The gala, the shopping trip on Sunday—each moment looms in my mind, not as obligations or entertainment, but as tantalizing opportunities. Excitement stirs within me, a feeling I haven't felt in a long while.

Curious, I open Junie's app and carefully enter my

info using a fake name. It's not about finding love, I remind myself. It's about understanding, dissecting, and knowing the apps I'm financing from the inside. If there's even the slightest chance I'll have to parade around in tights and a tutu, I'll be damned if I don't know precisely where I went wrong.

CHAPTER NINE

JUNIE

"Junie, this is like your *Pretty Woman* moment! You know, without the whole prostitute angle." Despite her illness, Liv's eyes shine with excitement, which even my fingerprint-covered screen can't diminish. I can almost smell the soup sitting in front of her, with its ribbon of steam reaching for the ceiling.

"Is this where you tell me you gave him to me?" I laugh, the sound of my boho dress rustling as I adjust it in the mirror. The fabric kisses my skin, as cool and light as a summer breeze. "This isn't some Cinderella story, and AJ isn't my Prince Charming. He's ... he's..." How do I describe him? On one hand, he feels like a boss, but that isn't accurate. He's an investor of sorts. He also seems like a friend but also a nemesis. "He defies labels. He's simply AJ."

"But he's picking you up, taking you shopping, and then escorting you to a gala," she says, her voice cracking with a little cough. "It's like something out of a movie."

The doorbell chimes, its sound bouncing off the walls of my cramped apartment, startling me. "That must be him. Wish me luck?"

"I'm just saying, if he hands you a necklace, I want to see the whole 'snap the jewelry box' thing happen," she teases, winking at me.

"I'll keep that in mind," I reply, ending the call with a smile and a wave, clicking the end button like a starting gun.

Opening the door, AJ's cologne fills my senses, a mixture of woodsy and fresh notes that are distinctly masculine. He's dressed casually yet impeccably in a tailored, button-up gray shirt that seems to shimmer with a soft texture, hugging his frame in all the right places. The sleeves are rolled up, revealing strong, sun-kissed forearms. His black jeans fit him just right, paired with stylish yet understated leather shoes. The corners of his eyes crinkle, and his lips twitch upward, as if he's holding back a laugh. There's a distant hum of traffic, but I can only focus on the man standing before me, offering a silent promise of adventure.

"You look ... colorful," he says, his eyes scanning my ensemble.

I twirl, letting my skirt billow. "Well, one of us has to make up for your fifty shades of grey."

"Fair point. But I like to think of it as a blank canvas. Makes your colors pop even more."

"Hopefully you won't look like you picked up a homeless woman off the street."

He laughs, a warm, rich sound that makes my cheeks

flush. "A homeless woman wouldn't be so clean." He leans forward and inhales. "Or smell so good."

"Thank you, I think." I step aside, the creak of the door accompanying his entry into my apartment. I watch as he takes in the cozy space, the smell of my vanilla-scented candles lingering in the air. He walks the perimeter from the living room to the kitchen. His gaze lingers a moment too long on the eviction notice pinned to the refrigerator. My breath catches, but he says nothing about it, his eyes meeting mine again.

"Are you ready?" he asks.

"Ready as I'll ever be," I say, my fingers relishing the cool leather of my purse as I snatch it up.

He holds the door open for me, and as we step outside, I'm surprised to see a sleek car waiting. Its engine hums, and the city sounds grow louder as the door closes behind us—a real *Pretty Woman* moment.

AJ guides me to the car and helps me inside. A flutter of excitement ripples through my belly as I sink into the luxurious leather seats. The scent of the new car mingles with AJ's cologne. We buckle up and pull away from my apartment in Tiburon.

As we approach the Golden Gate Bridge, I am entranced by the iconic structure, watching it through the closed windows. The rusty orange towers rise majestically against the clear blue sky and the waters of the bay sparkle beneath us.

"It never gets old, does it?" he remarks, a soft smile on his lips.

I shake my head, feeling connected to this place and

this moment. The bridge seems to symbolize the connection between my old life and the new possibilities that lie ahead in San Francisco.

This is not just a shopping trip. It's a journey into a world I've never experienced before, all thanks to the man who could turn my dreams into reality. The gentle hum of the car and the muted sounds of the city grow louder as we near our destination, and I feel a thrill of anticipation. What awaits us on the other side of this bridge is a mystery, but I'm ready to embrace it.

The drive to Saks near Union Square is filled with easy conversation. AJ's charm is disarming, his words flavored with humor and insight. I catch him glancing at me a few times, a thoughtful expression in his eyes. This is the first man I met. A man who could turn my bones to jelly.

Once inside Saks, the rich aroma of high-end perfume and fabric greets us. He escorts me upstairs, where he drops his credit card with a personal shopper named Avis. The experience becomes a whirlwind of colors, textures, and sensations.

The feel of silk and satin against my skin, the rustle of fabric as I twirl in front of the mirror, the clink of hangers, and the approving and disapproving nods from AJ blend into an exhilarating dance of fashion and fun.

At one point, I try on an outrageous number, a gown festooned with feathers and glitter that makes me feel like a peacock caught in a windstorm.

"What do you think?" I ask AJ, laughing as I strut awkwardly in the creation.

He raises an eyebrow, his lips quirking in amusement. "You look like a Macy's Thanksgiving Day Parade float that's come to life."

We both burst into laughter, and I change into the next option.

Several beautiful gowns follow, each one eliciting praise and critique.

"That one looks like a Grecian goddess's nightgown," he comments on one flowing, ethereal dress. "Beautiful, but not quite right for the gala."

Finally, I emerge from the dressing room in a fantastic gown. AJ's eyes meet mine, and his breath hitches. The look he gives me is pure, unfiltered desire. For a moment, everything else disappears.

I step toward him, but the high heels betray me, and I stumble forward. AJ's arms are there, catching me, holding me close. Our eyes lock, and the world falls away.

"You look perfect," he declares, his voice husky.

I gain my footing, glance at the price tag, and gasp. "Perfectly expensive, you mean."

He smiles, his eyes never leaving mine. "Perfection is priceless, don't you think?"

I try to match his intensity with humor. "Well, they certainly tried."

He laughs, then turns to the personal shopper. "We'll take it. And maybe a flat shoe option. I don't want her to die on our date."

Avis nods and goes to the counter to write up the ticket. But before I can say anything else, AJ's phone rings.

"Excuse me," he says, stepping away. I hear him answer, "Hello, Mother."

I take a moment to breathe, taking in the sights and sounds around me. The personal shopper's approving gaze, the rustle of expensive fabric, the soft murmurs of other customers. The real world comes crashing back.

When he returns, his expression is serious. "I need to talk to you about something else," he says, eyeing me with an intensity that makes me uneasy. "I noticed something at your apartment earlier."

"What?" I ask, my heart pounding in my chest.

"The eviction notice on your refrigerator. It's clear you need help."

My face heats, and I stammer, "It's a minor setback, but I can handle it. In fact, I have several interviews next week."

"Interviews? You're that confident you'll lose the challenge?"

"No, I just need a backup plan." My cheeks flush with a mix of embarrassment and indignation. I've always prided myself on being independent, on making my own way.

He shakes his head, a glimmer of resolve flashing in his eyes. "What I'm offering is not charity, but an extension of our business arrangement."

I frown, trying to figure out where he's going with this. "What kind of extension?"

"You've pretended to be my girlfriend once," he says. "The gala makes it twice. Let's agree to keep up the pretense until the app contest is over."

Overhearing our conversation, Avis pipes up, "You could do worse, honey. He's handsome, has real teeth, and money!"

I blush even deeper, and AJ rolls his eyes but smiles at the woman's comment. "Thank you for that glowing endorsement," he says to Avis, who winks and retreats to a safe distance.

Turning back to me, he continues, "I'm willing to pay you to pretend to be my girlfriend for more events. I also need someone for my cousin's wedding in Napa. It's a win-win situation. You get rid of that eviction notice, and I get a pleasant, witty companion for a few weeks. What do you think?"

"You want both days and nights?" I couldn't remember the exact line from the movie, but this was close. "That's going to cost you."

"I imagine it will be less than the wedding my mother would love to plan." He rubs his jaw. "I'll cover three months of rent. Besides, like she said, you could do worse."

A swirl of conflicting emotions churns within me. Pride battles with the stark reality of looming bills and an eviction notice. When I envisioned finding Mr. Right, it certainly didn't involve him offering me a job to save me from homelessness. Yet here we are. I've made worse choices, but I've also aimed for better.

After a moment's hesitation, a laugh escapes my lips. "You're far from the ideal catch, but I'll take the offer. Homelessness isn't on my bucket list."

He turns to the personal shopper. "She'll need a new

wardrobe for dinners, luncheons, black tie affairs, and a wedding. Put it on my card." He faces me. "I've got to go, but the car we arrived in will wait until you're ready to return home." He hands me the driver's business card. "Give Tony a twenty-minute heads up."

"Where are you going?" I ask, the unexpected shift in our conversation leaving me feeling off balance.

He gives me a look that's both professional and distant. "I have more business to take care of," he says smoothly. "Duty calls."

His words are like a splash of cold water, reminding me sharply that this isn't an actual date or relationship. It's a business deal, nothing more.

"I'll pick you up for the gala at six," he adds.

With that, he's gone, leaving me standing amidst the elegant clothes and glittering accessories, feeling elated and strangely empty. And for just a second, surrounded by all the glamour and glitz that's temporarily mine, I wish this was real.

CHAPTER TEN

AJ

I'm half-expecting to find Junie in bedazzled sneakers and a graphic T-shirt. But when she opens the door, time seems to freeze. There she is, a vision in a beautiful black dress that hugs her curves just right, the fabric shimmering like a night sky filled with stars. Her hair is simply styled with soft waves touching her shoulders, and her makeup is barely there with just a hint of mascara making her eyes sparkle with anticipation.

And her heels ... they're graceful and sleek, elevating her look to a level of sophistication I hadn't expected. My eyes widen, taking in the entirety of her transformation. "I must admit," I begin, my voice betraying a hint of awe, "I half-expected to find you in sequined Converse."

"Vans all the way, buddy." Junie laughs, the sound melodic and light. "Well, I figured I could at least make it from the car to my seat in these. After that, they're what Oprah calls 'sitting shoes.'"

I chuckle, appreciating her humor, but I'm battling to

keep it professional inside. This is a business arrangement, I remind myself, even as my heart pounds erratically.

Offering my arm, I help her navigate the stairs, feeling her grip tighten with each step down. "You're doing great," I say.

"Doing my best," she replies with a wry smile. "I only hope I can stay vertical tonight."

I grin but wrestle with emotions I haven't felt in a long time. Dressed like that, it's hard not to want her horizontal.

We make our way to the limousine waiting at the curb. Once settled inside, I reach for a chilled bottle of champagne from the built-in bar, and the car echoes with the cork's pop.

The golden bubbles dance in the crystal flutes as I pour and offer one to Junie, who accepts it with a gracious smile.

"Here's to a night we won't soon forget," I say, our glasses meeting in a celebratory clink.

"Unforgettable indeed," she agrees as she takes a sip.

The car glides through the streets, heading for the museum. I watch Junie as she looks out the window. Her profile is soft and elegant, and the way the light catches her hair makes it fire-like.

"So, what can I expect tonight?" she asks, turning to me with a curious look. "Other than struggling to stay upright in these shoes?"

I chuckle, appreciating her ability to keep things light.

"A lot of schmoozing and socializing," I say. "Networking with potential investors and rubbing elbows with the city's elite. And my mother."

"Yes, your mother." Junie's eyebrows rise. "I've done some thinking about tonight and your mom. Why do you let her manipulate you like this?" Junie asks with genuine curiosity, almost sounding like the therapist she was trained to be. "If you don't want to date, tell her." She points to her dress. "This is a mighty expensive ruse."

I look at her and laugh. "You might as well ask a hurricane to make a U-turn. Mom's a force of nature, category-five style. She's relentless. Sometimes, it's just easier to play the game."

Junie nods, but her eyes remain serious. "I see where you get it from. You can be quite intimidating yourself."

The boundaries between our business deal and a more personal connection grow increasingly hazy, leaving me grappling with a complex web of emotions. Junie is an enigma, a puzzle that intrigues every fiber of my being. On paper, she's not someone I'd typically be drawn to, yet her very essence captivates me. Her laughter, her keen observations, her playful spirit, and her audacity to challenge me—these qualities forge a connection I find impossible to overlook.

What's most disarming is her indifference to my wealth. She's the first woman I've encountered who acts as if my financial status is the least compelling thing about me. And yet, paradoxically, that very wealth could be her salvation.

Her uniqueness, the qualities that make her stand

out, are the very things pulling me toward her like a magnet. This newfound attraction unsettles me, particularly given the nature of our relationship. But it also invigorates me, awakening a curiosity and a sense of wonder I haven't experienced in ages.

"You think I'm intimidating?" I shift in my seat and sip my champagne. "I'm more like a teddy bear, really."

"I'd be curious to see what insect avatar my app would assign you. I bet you'd be a wasp or scorpion."

"I can't say I'm eager to try another dating app anytime soon. But who knows, maybe I am a scorpion."

I observe her. Inside, I'm battling a different truth. It assigned me an avatar I'd never expected—a ladybug. The description pricked my ego and hurt my masculinity. But even though it seemed contrary to everything I thought I was, I couldn't shake the idea that there might be truth in it. It said I was resilient, adaptable, social, collaborative, and effective. I can't argue with any of those attributes.

"What about you?" I ask, my voice teasing. "What would your app assign to you?"

Junie looks at me. "Oh, I couldn't possibly reveal that. It would spoil the mystery."

I laugh, enjoying her playful response. "Come on, you can't leave me hanging like that."

"Nope, my avatar is top secret," she says. "But I will say that it's not as glamorous as some."

"Dung beetle? Mosquito?"

"I'll never tell."

We settle into comfortable conversation, the Golden

Gate Bridge streaming past the windows as the limo whisks us toward the gala.

As we approach the San Francisco Museum of Modern Art, I'm drawn to the building's unique façade. The outside is marked by a wavy, white design, almost like a cloud. Enormous windows add to the look, and the light hitting the building makes it stand out. The museum's modern and creative appearance makes it the perfect place for tonight's event.

Junie's hand slips into mine as we exit the limousine, and I can't help but feel a sense of pride that she's my date.

We enter the grand hallway, and a sea of glittering gowns and tailored tuxedos greets us. The gentle hum of conversation fills the air, mingled with the soft notes of a string quartet playing in the background.

My mother appears through the crowd, elegant as always, but her eyes widen in genuine shock when she sees Junie. I can see her trying to reconcile the transformed woman in front of her with the person she had met before.

"Junie, you look beautiful," Mom says.

Junie looks down at her feet and then at my mother with a grin. "Why, thank you! I'm Cinderella if you swap the pumpkin carriage for a limo and ditch the wicked stepsisters." She winks, and I can't help but chuckle at her take on the evening. To me, it's just another night of obligation. To Junie, it's something far different. It's like a fairy tale.

Junie takes a step, her heel wobbling precariously.

She stumbles slightly, but I quickly catch her, steadying her with a firm hand at her waist.

"You'd think I'd have it down by now. I practiced all week walking in these, believe it or not. They're like stilts for your feet but less stable." She looks over at my mother, her expression a mix of admiration and curiosity. "How do you do it? Seriously, you glide around in heels like they're an extension of your legs. Is there a secret society I must join to master this skill?"

My mother, taking the comment in stride, leans closer. "Well, dear, it takes years of practice, a healthy dose of stubbornness, and you don't notice the pain after several martinis."

As the evening progresses, I proudly introduce Junie to everyone as my "girlfriend."

When a well-known socialite attempts to air-kiss both her cheeks, Junie misreads the cue and turns her head, resulting in a near-comical, real kiss on the lips. "Well, that's one way to make an introduction!" she giggles, both of them red-faced but laughing.

Every so often, she'd try to take a sip from her too-fancy cocktail, making a face each time as if she's just bitten into a sour lemon. "Who knew elegance could taste so ... challenging?" she'd say, drawing more laughs.

Then there's walking in her ambitious heels. She takes a step and stumbles slightly, but instead of getting flustered, she strikes an exaggerated ballet pose and announces, "Nailed it!"

I can't help but beam with pride and affection. It's her off-beat rhythm, her infectious energy, and her authentic self that lights up the room. Every now and then, I'd squeeze her hand or offer an encouraging smile. It's not just comfort, it's an acknowledgment of the unabashed brilliance she brings. There's an undeniable connection between us, and I can't help but wonder if everyone else feels its warmth too.

In a quiet moment, Mom asks, "Where are you practicing therapy now?"

"Oh, I quit seeing patients. Honestly, half the time they'd walk in, take one look at my mismatched socks or the coffee stain on my blouse, and ask if they should be counseling *me*! And the final straw? The day a woman brought her cactus and fern for 'group therapy.' Said they had interpersonal issues. I figured, if a cactus is having a better social life than me, maybe it's time for a career switch!"

"So, how are you putting that degree to use?"

"I craft questionnaires for apps, all steeped in psychology." She shakes her head. "One app, called Love Bug. It's a dating app."

My mother is speechless, or so it seems, but she rallies and asks, "An app? Are you working with AJ then?"

Junie looks at me as if to say, *Do you want to field this question?*

I gently squeeze her hand to let her know I've got this. "Junie's app is a finalist in our annual challenge."

Mom frowns. "Seems like that would be a conflict of interest, seeing as you're a couple." She puts emphasis on the word couple.

I shake my head. "Honestly, you can't convince me

that an algorithm can pick my soul mate, but if it wins, it does so on its own merit." Junie stiffens beside me, but I continue to explain. "Besides, I don't choose who wins. The public does this by purchasing the app. Each app gets the same budget and an ads team. It's out of my hands now. From this point forward, the numbers will speak for themselves."

"And how are the numbers looking?" Mom asks.

I pull out my phone to look at an app that tracks the finalists' progress, and I'm surprised to see that Junie's app is in the lead.

"Still early days, but Love Bug is more than just a blip on the radar." I turn to Junie and smile. "Congratulations."

She totters on her heels, and I touch my hand to her back to steady her, but she steps to the side and excuses herself to use the restroom.

Junie's hasty exit leaves a feeling of regret gnawing at me. I know I've hurt her by not believing in her app, and the silence she leaves behind speaks volumes.

My phone buzzes with a notification. When I look, I see that the Love Bug app has challenged me to find a piece of art that resonates with me. No doubt, it was triggered by my location.

"Tell Junie I'll be right back." I wander through the galleries, searching for something that calls to me. That's when I find it. "Boy with a Red Vest" by Paul Cézanne. It's not the most famous work, but something about it catches my eye.

The painting features a young boy seated and dressed

in a vivid red vest. His expression is contemplative, a mix of innocence and a hint of sadness. It strikes a chord deep within me. He's all dressed up and on display, but no one is paying attention to him.

As an only child, I often felt a deep sense of solitude. Growing up in a world of adults, business, and complex relationships, I yearned for something different. The boy's loneliness and introspective gaze remind me of the moments when I felt isolated, even in a crowd. I craved the playful laughter and chaos that other kids brought to their homes. My house echoed with silence rather than the joyous noise of siblings. Dinners were formal affairs, punctuated with discussions about stocks and world events, rather than playground squabbles or favorite cartoons. Weekends? They meant piano lessons, chess tutors, and business luncheons. The playgrounds, the scraped knees, and the thrill of a random water balloon fight were tales I knew only from books.

I pull out my phone, photograph the painting, and write in the app, "This painting resonates with me for portraying the isolation children often feel. It takes me back to my childhood when things were simpler yet often lonesome. A reflection of an only child's world." I may use a pseudonym, but my answers will be truthful. I owe the app at least that much, or maybe it's because I feel like I owe Junie.

I send it, feeling a connection with the painted boy. He's like a mirror, showing me a part of myself that I've kept hidden—someone yearning for more.

Returning to the event, I find Junie with my mother. I

reach out to her and take her hand. "I'm sorry. I didn't mean to hurt your feelings."

"You didn't. Like you said, the sales will speak for themselves."

I love her confidence. The quartet plays, and couples move to the center of the floor to dance. "Can I have this dance?"

She looks up at me. "You're quite the daredevil, huh? Attempting to dance with me is like trying to waltz with a shopping cart."

I chuckle at her humor and pull her close. "Well, I never back down from a challenge."

Her laughter, bright and musical, rings out as we step onto the dance floor. The world fades away as we sway to the music. Surprisingly, Junie's movements are fluid and graceful, and I enjoy the moment thoroughly.

As the song ends, I lean down and whisper in her ear, "You dance like a dream. Maybe you should create something like dance therapy."

She gives me a playful shove and says, "Or maybe you could quit judging apps and become a dance critic."

CHAPTER ELEVEN

JUNIE

As AJ pulls me close, leading us into a dance, I can't help but lose myself in the feel of his arms around me. There's something so solid and steady about him, a warmth that seeps through his touch and circles me like a comforting blanket. I glance up at him, catching his eyes, and something in his gaze makes my heart stutter.

This is a business transaction, I remind myself, trying to shake off the emotions threatening to bubble to the surface.

The music swells, and we move as one, our bodies finding a natural rhythm. It's intoxicating, this connection, and for a moment, I allow myself to pretend that it's real, that AJ and I are more than we are, but I know this is all make-believe. There's no prince, no glass slipper, and no pumpkin carriage.

All too soon, the song ends, and we make our way off the dance floor. AJ's mother approaches us, her eyes shining with approval as she bids us farewell.

"Don't forget about the wedding in Napa next weekend," she reminds AJ, her eyes shifting between us. "You two make such a lovely couple."

My lips curve into a smile, but it doesn't reach my eyes. A sharp twinge in my chest reminds me of the reality we're skirting.

The drive home is quiet, the energy from the evening slowly winding down. As the driver navigates the streets, I remember my phone buzzing earlier and figure it was Liv.

"I'm just going to check in with Liv," I tell him. "I'll only be a moment."

He nods, and I pull out my phone to find a notification from the Love Bug app. It's sent me a challenge to share my favorite piece of art, but since I'm no longer in the museum, I have to think about my favorite.

I smile as it comes to mind. It's a quirky and unexpected painting that has always resonated with me. "The Persistence of Memory" by Salvador Dalí. The melting clocks. The distorted reality. It all speaks to my inner impulsiveness and my love for the surreal.

Quickly, I search for an image online and snap a photo.

"What are you smiling about?" he asks, glancing over at me.

There is no way I will tell him I'm doing a dating app challenge. The man doesn't believe in the power of algorithms, and the experience would be lost on him, so I lie. "Liv wants to know how many of your toes I broke while dancing."

AJ laughs. "Tell her none. You can try harder at the wedding." His words are light and playful.

I set my phone down and kick out my feet. They are killing me. "High heels had to have been invented by a man."

I lean down and take off my shoes, and the minute I do, AJ shifts us both, so my feet are in his lap. As soon as his thumb moves up my instep, I moan. It probably sounds like the start of a climax, but honestly, it feels nearly as good. It starts low in my chest and rises as he works his way to my toes.

"Men designed them, but it was for men to make themselves taller," he says with some authority.

"How do you know that?" My soft moans continue as he moves to the other foot. I couldn't stop them if I tried.

"I got assigned a report in sixth grade on women's shoes. It was the worst moment of my life, but I got an A."

"It's because you're an overachiever."

"Why do anything if you're not going to do it right?"

As we pull up to my place, I find myself reluctant to say goodbye, to end this night filled with unexpected connections and genuine laughter. But reality waits, and I remind myself again that this is all a charade.

Still, as I climb out of the car with my heels in one hand, AJ's hand lingering on the other for just a moment too long, I can't help but wonder if there's more to this pretend relationship than either of us wants to admit.

He leans toward the driver, tells him to wait, and then walks me to my door. He takes my key and unlocks it, and leads me inside, shutting the door behind us.

I watch as AJ's eyes fall again on the eviction notice I have pinned to the refrigerator. It's a stark reminder of why I'm doing all of this. His gaze lingers on it.

He turns and looks at me, a long, searching look that makes my heart skip a beat. "You know," he says, his voice softer now, "you're beautiful. Not just tonight, but always."

Before I can respond, he steps closer, his eyes fixed on mine. He reaches up, brushing a stray curl to the side, his touch gentle but firm. I drop my shoes, and they hit the ground with a thud. At that moment, the distance between us is gone.

He leans down, and his lips meet mine in a gentle kiss, a mere brush, a question asked and answered. His mouth is warm, and I feel a shiver run down my spine as he deepens the kiss, his lips moving over mine with a slow, deliberate sensuality that leaves me breathless.

His hands find their way to my waist, pulling me closer, and the hard planes of his body press against mine. I reach up to touch his face, my fingers tracing the line of his jaw, feeling the slight stubble that adds to the delicious friction of the moment.

The kiss grows more intense, more passionate, our tongues exploring each other in a dance as old as time yet as new as if we're the first to discover it. My heart pounds, my blood sings in my veins, and all I can think about is how right this feels, how perfect.

His taste is intoxicating, a blend of wine and desire. I lose myself in the sensations, the soft moans and sighs that escape both of us as the kiss continues. His hands move up my back, stoking the wildfire within me.

Time seems to lose meaning as we continue to discover each other, every touch a revelation, every moment building on the last until I feel like I'm standing on the edge, teetering between control and surrender.

And then, as abruptly as it began, he pulls away. He looks at me, eyes wide and filled with something I can't quite name.

"Why did you kiss me?" What I really want to ask is, why did you stop?

"I was wondering if I'd like it."

"And?"

"I do, but I shouldn't," he says, his voice barely above a whisper. "I shouldn't have done that." He glances at the eviction notice, his expression now resolute. "I'll take care of that." He walks over to the refrigerator and pulls it free, tucking it into his pocket before striding to the door and walking out.

I'm left standing there, breathless, and bewildered, my lips tingling from his touch and my body aching for him. The night is over, yet something has changed. But for now, all that's left is the silence and the lingering taste of a kiss that promised so much more.

With shaky fingers, I text Liv, asking if she's up. Almost instantly, my phone rings, and I answer, her voice bright and cheerful in my ear.

"Spill! How was it? Details, girl!"

I step into my bedroom and trade my elegant gown for the comfort of flannel pajamas while recounting the night's events to Liv. The laughter, the connection, the unexpected kiss. I describe it all, reliving the moments as I speak, feeling excitement and confusion.

"Are you sure this is all pretend?"

"It has to be," I reply, trying to convince myself as much as her. "It's just business." My phone buzzes with a new notification, and I see that Love Bug has revealed the avatar of my match for me. I click on it, my heart racing as I see it's a ladybug, bright and cheerful.

"Liv, I think my match was at the event. His avatar is a ladybug."

"What? A ladybug? Are you sure it's not AJ?" she asks.

I laugh, finding the notion absurd. "AJ, a ladybug? No way. He'd translate into something far more fierce."

We talk a bit more, my mind still whirling from the night's events. I finally hang up and settle into bed, the paradox of AJ's tenderness tonight juxtaposed with my assumptions about what kind of bug he would be nagging at me. I conclude that there is no way he and I are a match. He is everything I'm not. He's suave, confident, and graceful, while I'm quirky and prone to stumbling. He's a successful man, commanding attention with a glance while I'm just trying to find my place in the world. He knows exactly what he wants and how to get it while I'm navigating through life, guided by gut feelings.

I turn my thoughts to the ladybug avatar on the app and wonder who it could be. Who at the gala would have been paired with me, a fire ant? Who sees the world as I do, despite the differences in our avatars? I recall the faces and conversations, trying to piece together clues. Was it a brief interaction, a fleeting connection that the app somehow caught? I long to know who's behind the avatar, eager to explore this mysterious connection.

As I drift off to sleep, the memories of the night swirl in my mind. It was magical, yet here I am, alone, wondering if I missed a chance at finding my true love while pretending to be AJ's.

CHAPTER TWELVE

AJ

I stare at the avatar on my phone. It's a fire ant. The matching system of Love Bug has paired me with this person, who chose "The Persistence of Memory" by Salvador Dalí as their favorite painting. There's a short description explaining why it's important to her, something about its quirkiness and unexpectedness resonating with her love for the surreal.

Junie. The thought springs into my head, and I quickly shake it away. It can't be her. I scroll through the app, reading the reasons behind the painting choice. Still, the more I read, the more I think of Junie's free-spirited nature, infectious laugh, and the sparkle in her eyes.

No, I tell myself, forcefully pushing the idea aside. We're too different, too opposite in every conceivable way. I'm all about control, precision, and success. She's about intuition, spontaneity, and stumbling through life. Besides, I don't believe in this app's power to find true love through algorithms.

The phone slips from my grasp, landing with a soft thud on the desk. The very concept of true love seems ludicrous to me. Fifty percent of marriages end in divorce. How is that possible if people are marrying their perfect matches? And how many people really find their spouses through an app like this?

From my office, I gaze down at the bustling city below. The streams of people look almost insect-like from this height, scurrying through their daily routines. How many of them are blissfully happy? How many are merely content? How many, like me, question the idea that a person can complete you?

My eyes drift back to my office, taking in the sleek lines of the furniture, the meticulously organized bookshelves, and the high-tech gadgets I surround myself with. They represent control, order, and a life defined by logic and reason. But this room has an emptiness, a hollowness that no success can fill. I miss having someone special who understands me, laughs at my jokes, and stands by me. I miss the connection, the intimacy. But true love? It's a fairy tale, a made-up concept to sell romance novels and movies.

Yet, something about Junie tugs at me, something beyond our charade. I can't shake off the memory of her lips, the taste of the unexpected kiss, the way her body responded to my touch. It's all pretend, a game we're playing. Isn't it?

I shake my head, feeling a pang of something I can't quite identify. I don't believe in love, I remind myself. Not in the kind that lasts forever.

The phone buzzes again, a new notification from Love Bug. I ignore it, pushing it aside. The fire ant is just a symbol, a random match. It's not Junie. Even if it is, we're not meant to be.

With a sigh, I get up from my desk, ready to face the day, prepared to bury the strange emotions that have welled up within me. It's all a game, a business transaction, a necessary smokescreen so I don't end up in a real charade of a marriage. Today, I've got business to take care of. There's no room for feelings, for dreams, for fairy tales.

I look at the phone one last time before leaving the office and striding down the corridor, my thoughts a turbulent whirlpool of confusion. As I approach the office break room, I see Henry pouring himself a coffee. His eyes narrow as he spots me, and he tilts his head.

"You look like you've seen a ghost," he says, handing me a cup.

I take the coffee and grimace. "Or kissed one."

Henry's eyebrows shoot up, his interest piqued. "Oh?"

I find myself telling him about the kiss with Junie, the words spilling out in a torrent. Henry listens intently.

"I knew something was going on between you two," he says. "I could feel the chemistry."

"Chemistry? No, no," I say, shaking my head. "It's just a charade. We're pretending to be together, so my mom doesn't have me married to Camilla by the end of summer. It's nothing more."

Henry leans back, studying me. "Is it really pretend? You two seem to click despite the differences."

I roll my eyes. "Click? We're like oil and water, complete opposites. How could we possibly be a real match?"

"Opposites attract," Henry says. "You know that, right?"

I dismiss the clichéd notion. "That's just a saying. In reality, it doesn't work that way. Just look at us—she's carefree and impulsive. I'm methodical and focused. We would drive each other insane in a real relationship."

Henry sips his coffee. "Maybe that's exactly what you need. Someone to shake you up, challenge you, make you see things differently."

I frown, uneasy with the idea. It's not that simple. Love is a complicated, unpredictable beast, one I'm not willing to wrestle with, especially not with someone like Junie. Our differences would tear us apart, I'm sure of it.

"We need to head out for that business lunch at Scoma's," I say, changing the subject. "Let's go." I put my coffee in the sink and walk away.

As we leave the office, Henry's words echo in my mind, a haunting reminder of something I can't quite put my finger on. Opposites attract? Perhaps. But attraction doesn't mean compatibility, and compatibility is what truly matters. Isn't it?

I shake my head, pushing the thoughts away. This is business, not romance. There's no room for such senti-mentality. Yet, as I step into the elevator, I can't help but feel a nagging doubt, a whisper of uncertainty that refuses to be silenced.

THE CITY PASSES in a blur as Henry and I make our way to Scoma's. We navigate through traffic, lost in thought, the radio playing softly in the background.

As we pull into the parking lot, Henry turns the volume down and looks at me. "You really don't believe in true love, do you?"

I grip the door handle, my knuckles turning white. "It's not about belief, Henry. It's about facts. Half of marriages end in divorce. How is that possible if you're marrying the one? It's a myth. A fantasy."

He leans back in his seat, folding his arms. "Maybe those people didn't find their perfect match. Maybe they settled. You can't use statistics to judge something as complex as love."

He cuts the engine, and I unbuckle my seatbelt. "That's the point. Love is multifaceted and unpredictable. It's not something you can find through a formula. Most people who marry don't use an app. They meet, they connect, and they choose to be together. But that doesn't guarantee anything."

Henry opens the car door and steps out. "That's what makes it beautiful, AJ. The uncertainty, the risk, the choice. That's what love is."

I follow him out of the car, my mind still wrestling with the concept. "I admit, I miss having someone special in my life." The words catch in my throat. "But the idea of finding the one? It's ludicrous. It doesn't exist. You have to find the one you don't want to murder after a decade of togetherness."

He laughs and places a reassuring hand on my shoulder. "Don't be so cynical. Maybe you just haven't found the right person yet."

We enter the restaurant, the initial aroma of seafood filling the air in a potent wave. To some, it might be a delightful scent, a promise of freshly caught delicacies. It's a complex mixture that's both enticing and unsettling. The briny tang of the ocean is mingled with the rich butter and garlic being sautéed in the kitchen, creating a sensory collage that's hard to define.

As we're shown to our table, my mind struggles to reconcile these conflicting smells, reflecting my tangled emotions about love and connection. But then, something else catches my attention, something far more potent than any culinary aroma. I glimpse a familiar redhead through the window. And on closer inspection, I see Junie, her fiery hair shining in the sunlight. She's talking to a vendor below—a fishmonger dressed in a T-shirt, apron, and rubber boots. Her smile is dazzling. Is she flirting with him? My heart skips a beat, and a sudden pang of jealousy shoots through me, more intense and unexpected than any flavor or fragrance in the restaurant.

I shake my head, trying to focus on the meeting ahead. This is important. Distractions—be it Junie or a fire ant avatar—can't afford a seat at this table. Love is a game I'm not willing to play.

But as we sit down and wait for our client to arrive, I can't help but glance out the window again. Junie is still there, laughing and smiling. A wave of possessiveness crashes over me, an irrational urge to stake my claim. I wrench my gaze away, yet the vision of Junie and the fishmonger lingers, a haunting reminder of what I'm denying myself.

The clients arrive, and we dive into business, but I find concentrating hard. My thoughts keep drifting back to Junie, to the connection we share, to the doubts and uncertainties that plague me, to what in the hell is she doing with that guy?

Henry's voice yanks me back from my thoughts. "AJ, Carl was just asking if we're finished?" We were fine-tuning the deal, and I spaced out. I look at Henry. "I'll leave you to iron out the details with Henry." Rising, I grasp Carl's hand firmly. "An urgent matter calls for my attention."

Henry studies me, his eyes narrowing. "Right. That issue with the dating app developer?"

"That's the one." I push in my chair. "You okay here?"

Henry didn't need me for anything else, so I rush outside in search of Junie. Just last night, she was kissing me. What is she doing here? I burst out of the restaurant, my mind reeling, my heart pounding. The world blurs around me as I walk toward her, my feet moving of their own accord.

I reach them, and the fishmonger looks up, surprised. Junie turns, her eyes wide, her face pale.

"Junie," I growl, my voice filled with betrayal and confusion. "What are you doing here?"

Her eyes widen as she opens her mouth to speak, but no words come out.

The fishmonger takes a step back, confusion written across his face. "Dude, she ate a sea urchin."

I stand there, my chest heaving, waiting for an answer, for an explanation, while Junie falls to the ground in a heap.

JUNIE

Consciousness returns to me slowly, my eyes fluttering open to find AJ's face inches from mine. Confusion reigns for a moment, and then I remember the fish stand, the free sample of the urchin, the allergic reaction. My thigh aches, and I shift my hand to find the sore spot, only to have AJ catch my wrist gently.

"Hands off," he cautions, worry etching his voice. "The EpiPen most likely left a bruise."

I blink at him, my mind still fuzzy, and then I notice the paramedics bustling around us. AJ insists I get checked out by a doctor, but I refuse. The last thing I need is a hospital bill. Girls without jobs don't have insurance. AJ discusses my condition with the paramedics, asking if it's safe for me to go home. Relief washes over me as one of them reassures AJ that I'm stable. They provide him with instructions, listing things he should watch for over the next several hours. I catch snippets of their conversation, but I'm more focused on AJ's eyes, his face, the way he's holding me like I'm something precious.

"Why are you here?" AJ asks once the paramedics have left us alone. His voice is light, but I detect a note of concern. "Was it something I said, or perhaps something I did?" He gives the fishmonger a look that I can't decipher but resembles annoyance. "Was it the kiss?"

I laugh, surprised by his comment. "You mean the one you wanted to forget as soon as it happened?"

He hangs his head. "I was out of line. Kisses weren't part of our deal or expected."

"It's the unexpected that makes life interesting." I shift from his hold and take a seat on a nearby bench. AJ follows me, leaving the fishmonger behind.

"You sound like Henry."

I smile. "I like Henry."

His eyes widen. "As in *like* him, like him?"

I laugh, picking at a splinter on the bench. "No, I think he's a nice person."

AJ sits beside me, and he's so close his thigh touches mine. The cool ocean breeze doesn't even phase me because that one touch has heated my entire body.

"He's my best friend."

I turn to face him, our eyes locking. "Did you tell him about the kiss?"

He hesitates just a beat too long. "I did."

"And?" I prompt, curiosity getting the better of me.

"He didn't have much to say."

My lips quirk into a smirk. "Well, Liv got an earful from me."

His interest piqued, he leans in. "And?"

"She had a lot to say, but it doesn't matter. It was just a kiss."

He looks away, gazing out to the horizon. "But it meant something."

I swallow hard, as his words press in on me. "Maybe. But it shouldn't, right?"

He doesn't answer immediately. Instead, he taps on his phone briefly, then looks at me. "So, what brings you here? Was it the app? Did it send you here for a match?"

"No." I'd never tell him that I'm using the app. "While you're paying my rent, I still need to eat and pay for utilities," I respond, matching his tone. "You may be my pretend boyfriend, but that doesn't cover everything. I was here for a job interview. I told you I had a few scheduled."

"It looked like more." He raises an eyebrow. "You could do much better than that guy, you know."

"That guy's name is Grant." His words spark something inside me. "Are you jealous?"

His head snaps back for just a second before he composes himself. "Just looking out for you," he says, but the expression in his eyes tells me otherwise. "Grant stood there and stared at you as you hit the ground. You'd be dead if I hadn't called for help."

The mood between us flattens, but I sense an undercurrent of something more underneath it.

Then, I realize the reality of the situation, the danger I had been in, and the man who had been there for me through it all. The connection I feel to AJ is no longer just a charade, but I'll keep that to myself.

As AJ helps me stand and escorts me to a waiting car, his touch is gentle, his concern genuine. He's treating me like I'm something delicate, something to be cared for. The drive to my apartment is filled with questions, ensuring I'm okay and comfortable.

Once inside, his eyes scan the room, taking in my futon with its orange and pink pillows, the big cable-knit throw, and the pictures of Jobs, Musk, and Winfrey hanging on the walls.

"You need a job? Why don't you have an emergency fund?" His eyebrows knit together as if the possibility is absurd.

"An emergency fund? Please, if I had a stash of cash lying around, I wouldn't be hustling here with you." I cross my arms, meeting his gaze head-on. "Besides, every penny went into breathing life into that app. And until it wins, I have to make a living. Pretend relationships don't pay the bills or put food on the table."

He chuckles, loosening his tie and unbuttoning his coat, making himself at home. "I still think you're too good for Grant, the fish guy."

"He's a nice guy." I tease him, "And yet, you're jealous."

"I'm not," he protests, but the spark in his eye betrays him.

"I think you are," I insist, a playful smile tugging at my lips.

He shakes his head, smiling back, but doesn't argue

further. Instead, he heads to the kitchen, calling over his shoulder, "How about I order some takeout? Something filled with shellfish."

"Are you trying to kill me?"

He returns, mock offense in his eyes. "It might be easier than convincing my mother we broke up."

"Are we breaking up already?" My heart thuds.

"Nope, we've got a few weeks left to our deal. Let's get through the wedding, and then we'll call it quits."

The thought of never seeing him again was heartbreaking, but it was the deal, and I was getting rent out of it.

He pulls up an app on his phone. "Do you like beef with broccoli?"

I nod. "And orange chicken and egg drop soup. I like it all."

He places an order. "Dinner should be here in about thirty minutes. I made sure they didn't include any shellfish."

"Fabulous, I'll live another day." I plop onto the futon, lean back, and pull the throw to my chin. "Why were you at Fisherman's Wharf? Dating app?" The app doesn't always give the match the same challenge but often triggers it when the match is nearby. When my challenge came in, I thought it might be Grant because he smiled at me and flirted, even though I was there for an interview.

AJ shakes his head. "I'm not on the app. I told you. I don't believe in them."

Sadness fills me, but I push it aside. There's no need

to feel down about something that isn't meant to be. And if AJ is telling the truth and isn't using the app, then it very well could have been Grant, but could I fall for a man who didn't save the day when I needed him to? So far, the only knight in shining armor has been AJ, and he's a tarnished one at best.

His phone rings, and for the next twenty minutes, AJ excuses himself while I relive the terror of the allergic reaction in my mind.

My doorbell rings, the food arrives, and we settle in for a comfortable evening. There's a shift in our relationship, but I can't put it into words.

The tension, the connection, it's all there, simmering beneath the surface, and I can't help but wonder where this is leading, even as I tell myself it's all make-believe.

We dig into the delicious-smelling Chinese food, a sense of ease settling over us as we enjoy our meal. I watch AJ as he samples the orange chicken, his appreciation evident in his expression. The scene feels almost couple-like, and I enjoy his company more than I expected.

"Did you know," he begins, his eyes narrowed in thought, "that you were allergic to shellfish?"

"Yes." I hold up my chopsticks. "But that was a sea urchin. I had no idea it was considered shellfish. The guy offered me a sample and told me it tasted like butter. Who doesn't like butter?"

"Did it taste like butter?"

I made a face. "The texture is buttery, but the taste is like sucking on seaweed straight from the shore."

His lips quirk. "Got a lot of experience with that?"

I shake my head, a little embarrassed. "No, but it's what I'd imagine it would taste like."

The more time I spend with AJ, the more I realize there's more to him than I thought. He's not just the polished, sophisticated businessman I see in public. He's also sweet and surprisingly down-to-earth.

As we finish our meal, his eyes flick to the television in the corner of the room. "How about a movie?"

"You don't have to stay. I'm sure I'll be fine."

"Nonsense, I promised the EMTs that I'd look after you for a few hours. I'm not one to shirk my responsibilities."

How I wish he was here because he wants to be and not because of some silly sense of duty.

"What do you have in mind?"

He grins, scrolling through the available options. "How about *Pretty in Pink*? It's a classic."

I raise an eyebrow, surprised by his choice but pleased, nonetheless. "I love that movie! But isn't it a bit too ... romantic for you?"

He shrugs, his face lighting up with a boyish grin. "I've been known to enjoy a rom-com now and then. They generally prove how silly love is."

We settle in to watch the movie, and I can't help but steal glances at AJ as he becomes engrossed in the story. I see him smile at the romantic scenes and frown at the conflicts.

As the movie progresses, our conversation shifts to the characters and their dilemmas. He seems genuinely engaged in the storyline, and I tease him about liking chick flicks.

"I bet she thought it was a perfect love," he says.

"You really think it wouldn't work out?" I challenge, pointing at the screen where the two main characters face the social barriers that divide them.

He shrugs, leaning back on the futon and propping an arm behind his head. "It's all Hollywood fantasy, Junie. In real life, there are practical considerations. Money, social standing, family expectations. They matter."

I laugh, shaking my head at his cynicism. "You're just too cynical. True love conquers all."

He gives me a sidelong glance. "Is that what you believe?"

I open my mouth to respond, a witty reply on the tip of my tongue. But instead, I find myself pausing, caught off guard by the sincerity in his eyes. It's a question that strikes at something deeper, something I've been wrestling with myself.

"Well," I say, unsure of how to respond. "Maybe not conquers all, but it's certainly powerful. Don't you believe in love?"

He's quiet for a moment, his expression thoughtful. With a heavy exhale, he turns his gaze elsewhere. "Love is a fairy tale, and I don't buy into those stories."

I'm taken aback by his response, struck by the raw honesty in his voice. "But why?" I press, leaning closer, genuinely curious. "Why don't you believe in it?"

He hesitates, his eyes flicking to mine, then away.

"Life has a way of teaching you lessons. Sometimes those lessons are harsh."

I watch him, seeing the sadness in his eyes, and suddenly, I understand. There's a story there, a heartbreak that he's not ready to share. And I realize that, despite our playful banter and easy camaraderie, we still don't know much about each other.

The rest of the movie passes in thoughtful silence, each of us lost in our thoughts. As the credits roll, I feel a pang of regret, wishing I could reach out and comfort him, reassure him that love is real and worth believing in.

Instead, I offer him a small smile, grateful for our time together and silently hoping he might someday believe in love again.

AJ glances at his watch. "I should probably head out. You need your rest, and I have an early day tomorrow."

A wave of disappointment hits me. The evening has been so enjoyable, and the thought of it ending deflates me a little. But I nod, standing up from the futon.

He looks at the pictures on my wall and reaches for his coat. "What's with the eclectic collection?"

"Inspiration," I say, thrilled he's taking an interest. "They've all faced challenges, defied the odds, and succeeded."

His eyes hold mine, a mix of intensity and curiosity. "Earlier, you mentioned needing a job. I'll ensure you have what you need until the end of the contest."

I shake my head and say, "You've already left enough Chinese food to last a week. And when I said I like it all, that didn't mean you needed to order everything on the menu."

Ignoring my protest, he takes out his wallet and hands me several hundred-dollar bills. "This should get you through the week. We can sort out the rest when I see you this weekend."

Reluctantly, I fold the money into my palm. "It's a loan. I'll pay you back."

He suddenly looks me up and down. "Why didn't you wear any of the clothes I bought you to your interview?"

I glance at my floral button-down and black pants. "Those are for when I'm with you."

A momentary smile graces his lips before it fades. "They're yours to use as you wish."

"They felt too extravagant for a seafood market interview."

His expression shifts, puzzled. "Why even consider a job like that? With your degree and a shellfish allergy, no less?"

"Jobs don't grow on trees, AJ," I say, a defensive edge to my voice. "It's what was available."

He gives me a look that's both understanding and sad. "You should be doing more with your skills, not wasting them on something like that."

Before I can respond, he glances back at my wall art and says, "You know, I would've pegged you as more of a Dalí girl."

My heart skips a beat. Is his mention of that piece

just a coincidence, or a Love Bug reveal? Just as I start to say something, he leaves.

My mind races. Could he be the one? But then reality sets in, as it always does. After all, in my world, there's no room for fairy tales. My eyes linger on the closed door, and for a fleeting second, the "what if" haunts me.

CHAPTER FOURTEEN

AJ

As the Porsche 911 glides effortlessly along the Tiburon streets, the smoothness of the ride feels like a mockery of the emotional turbulence churning inside me. The car may offer an easy, effortless journey but won't cushion the bumps and jolts waiting for me at my cousin's wedding. Worse, the sister of the bride is my ex-fiancée. It's a tangled web of almost-in-laws and broken promises that no high-speed engine can outrun. But Junie, she's like a bright thread in this knotted mess—effortlessly vibrant and curiously strong.

I cut the engine and head up to her apartment. She's absolutely stunning when she opens the door, draped in one of the elegant dresses I'd bought her. Her eyes light up at the sight of me but then quickly cloud with confusion as she takes in my casual attire.

"You look great," she says, hesitating. "Are we leaving now?"

"You look amazing, too," I reply. "But you know that the wedding festivities span the whole weekend, right?"

She blinks. "Weekend? I thought the ceremony was today."

"Ah, no. That's tomorrow. Today is just the warm-up." I watch her eyes widen as the implications sink in. "Do you want to pack some more stuff?"

She pales, then blushes. "Uh, come in. I'll be just a moment."

I step inside, closing the door behind me. She rushes off like a whirlwind and I stand in the hallway where I can see her. She tugs a garish flower-patterned, oversized suitcase from beneath her bed and flings it open, stuffing it with a riot of clothing. The bag looks like it was designed by a clown or perhaps a five-year-old let loose in a fabric store.

She hops around, kicking off her heels, and she disappears into the bathroom to change into slacks. When she re-enters, she slips into patent leather flats, glancing down and shifting her feet. "Wow, these are comfy."

"At $400 a pair, they better offer your feet a full spa experience," I say.

She laughs. "If these flats were any more expensive, they'd need to come with their own financial advisor. This is a one-time indulgence and only because you bought them."

Her zany packing extravaganza and sharp humor dissolve the tension I didn't even realize was building in me. I'm struck again by how she does that—takes an awkward or stressful situation and spins it into something light, even joyful.

She zips up her suitcase, which looks ready to burst at the seams, and rolls it toward the door. "Okay, let's get this show on the road."

As she drags the bag through her apartment, I can't help but marvel at the juxtaposition between it and the woman pulling it—a woman who's managed to add an unexpected spark of life to an otherwise daunting weekend.

We lug her bag down the stairs and into the car. The trunk barely closes over the top, but somehow, we make it work. I help her in and then round the vehicle to slide back into my seat. I think of the weekend ahead.

The ride to Napa stretches longer than the miles on the odometer, each moment heavy with silent thoughts. The car's interior is plush, yet it can't fully cushion the unaddressed questions that have accumulated since we left the city. We're a couple hours into the drive when Junie finally breaks the silence.

"So, where exactly are we staying?" she asks, thumbing through playlists on her phone.

"At the winery," I answer. "There's an estate on the grounds. Rooms have been booked for everyone."

"For everyone?"

"Well, for family and close friends."

She hesitates before taking the plunge. "And where am I staying?"

It hits me that I haven't thought this through as much as I should have. But the prospect of sharing a room doesn't sound bad. At all. "With me," I say, keeping my voice steady. "I'll take care of it."

Junie looks over, her eyes narrowing, then softening. "Alright, if you say so."

She leans back in her seat, eyes wandering out the window as we pass through rolling hills and sprawling vineyards. I remember the look on her face last night when I mentioned Dalí. Her eyes had widened, her expression changing like she'd discovered something new—something positive. I find myself questioning whether the algorithm of the dating app is matching us perfectly or if we're subconsciously aligning in real life.

We roll into the winery estate in the early afternoon, its sprawling landscape drenched in a golden light. The rows of grapevines, the grand mansion, the rustic guest-houses—everything comes into view like a scene from a luxury travel brochure.

"Wow," Junie says, stepping out of the car and looking around like she's landed in a different universe. "This is ... amazing."

"It is something," I admit. Her wide-eyed wonder makes me appreciate the familiar sights anew. Maybe this weekend, with Junie's laughter filling the spaces where my reservations lay, won't be such an ordeal after all. Perhaps it's just the beginning of something unexpected, something extraordinary.

As we pull up to the luxurious estate, my mother is the first to greet us, her face lighting up when she sees Junie. "You made it! We're about to take a tour of the vineyard. Why don't you both join us?"

I glance at Junie, who seems as enthusiastic as one can be about grapes and soil. "What about our bags?" she asks. "Shouldn't we check in first?"

My cousin, ever the laid-back vintner, waves a hand dismissively. "Oh, don't worry about that. You can settle in later. The vines won't wait, but the room will."

Reluctantly, I agree. As we tour the vineyard, tasting samples from barrels and listening to passionate speeches about soil pH levels, I find myself more at ease than antic-ipated. Perhaps it's Junie's genuine interest in the wine-making process, or maybe it's the way her laughter makes even the most mundane details seem fascinating.

Either way, I'm in a significantly better mood when we sit down for the rehearsal dinner. That is, until I see her—my ex, Sophia, seated right next to me.

Rehearsal dinners are not my scene. It is an appetizer course to the main matrimonial feast but filled with just as much awkward conversation and unsolicited advice. The long banquet table is adorned with flickering candles and delicate floral arrangements. While I turn my back to Sophia to give all my attention to Junie, I can't shake the sensation of Sophia's stare—piercing through me as if trying to freeze the newfound warmth I've discovered tonight.

"So, AJ, you haven't introduced me to your lovely date," Sophia begins, her voice oozing sweetness that I no longer find endearing.

"Junie, meet Sophia," I manage, my voice colder than I intend, but probably just reflecting some of the ice I feel from her glare.

Junie greets Sophia with a polite smile and a quick "hello," but her eyes shift toward me as if sensing the tension in the air.

Sophia's eyes narrow slightly as she sizes up Junie. "So, Junie, how did you and AJ meet? He's usually so secretive about his love life."

Before I can jump in with a fabricated tale, Junie smiles and says, "Well, let's just say our connection was immediate. Isn't that right, honey?"

Her words, tinged with a playful vagueness, remind me of the charged atmosphere of our initial meeting at the bar. Intrigued, I decide to go along with her. "Indeed, our connection was ... remarkably in sync from the moment we met."

Sophia shifts uncomfortably in her seat, a flash of annoyance in her eyes. "Connection, huh? That's a word AJ rarely uses."

"Times change," I say, squeezing Junie's hand under the table for added effect.

"And people do, too," Junie adds. She takes a sip of her wine, her eyes meeting mine momentarily, silently conveying a well-done.

Sophia clears her throat, visibly stumped by our united front. "Well, love is just fascinating, isn't it? One moment, you think you've found the one, and the next moment, you're sitting beside them at dinner, merely as friends."

"Or less," I counter, feeling bolder thanks to Junie's unexpected but welcome support.

Junie says, "Love isn't just about finding the right

person. It's also about *being* the right person. You have to be ready to appreciate what's in front of you." Her eyes lock onto mine as she says this, and I can't help but feel she's talking to me as much as she is to Sophia.

Sophia sighs dramatically, clearly defeated for the moment. "Well, I wish you both the best of luck. Love is a challenging game."

"Who says we're playing games?" Junie delivers the final blow with a radiant smile.

Sophia retreats into her wine glass, and I look approvingly at Junie.

During the dinner, my phone buzzes. I stare down to see a notification from the dating app. "Share a secret with your match." Not feeling like sharing much more than a glass of wine with anyone, I bury my phone in my pocket, but wonder if my "match" will get the same question, and if so, what will she share? I glance at Junie to see if she's received a notification, but she sits there smiling, making me wonder if I've got it all wrong. Sophia's phone buzzes and my heart sinks into the pit of my stomach. What if the app matched me to her? But she glances at her phone and tucks it away.

After a lingering dessert and multiple toasts, the rehearsal dinner winds down. I take Junie's hand, pulling her away from the crowd. We walk, and our footsteps are soft on the manicured pathways that snake through the winery grounds.

"You've been quiet," she observes.

"So have you," I say.

She smiles, a look that says she knows she's caught

me. "Alright, out with it. Who's Sophia? And why did you look like you'd swallowed a sour grape every time she spoke?"

I pause, weighing my words. Then I decide to let it out, to share a part of me I've kept locked away. "Sophia and I were engaged once, but she left me for another man. That's why I have trouble believing in ... all this." I wave my hand at the romantic setting around us, the glowing fairy lights, the promise of forever that a wedding implies. "We were three weeks from the wedding when she slept with one of my best friends."

Junie gasps. "Henry?"

"No, another good friend named Derek."

She makes a sound in her throat like a growl and then laughs. "I've never met a Derek I've liked."

"I liked him until then."

"He was no friend." Junie's eyes soften, and her earlier vivaciousness is replaced by a compassionate stillness. She doesn't offer clichés or empty reassurances. She squeezes my hand and says, "Thank you for telling me."

In that moment, something extraordinary happens. It's as if a yoke has been lifted off my shoulders, and a wall I've carefully constructed brick by brick crumbles into dust. I'm flooded with an unexpected sense of relief and vulnerability. I realize how starved I've been—not just for touch, but for understanding, a genuine connection beyond profiles, algorithms, and calculated interactions. The air between us thickens with an electricity I can no longer ignore. And then, before I can second-guess myself and build another wall, I lean in and kiss her. The sensation is like finding water in a desert, and I drink it in as if I've been parched for years. Standing together on this secluded vineyard path, surrounded by rows of grapevines that stretch toward the horizon, the world around us seems to fade away. With Junie's lips pressed to mine, I'm held fast by a feeling I can't quite define, like finding a missing piece of a puzzle you didn't even know was incomplete.

The earthy scent of the vineyard soil, the distant aroma of blossoming flowers, and the crisp evening air all blend seamlessly with the unique fragrance that is purely Junie. As I breathe her in, I'm intoxicated in a way that no wine, however fine, has ever managed to achieve.

The kiss isn't just physical. It transcends that, becoming its own emotional language. All my reservations and doubts evaporate for a few incredible moments, leaving nothing but an extraordinary sense of possibility and rightness.

The press of her lips, the light catch of her breath, and the subtle way she leans into me. It tells me unequivocally that she's just as affected by this connection as I am. And for a few moments, everything complicated turns incredibly simple.

It's a sweet release, a moment where the past and its jagged edges seem to blur, replaced by the thrilling sensation of the present. We're still caught in that moment when we hear a subtle throat-clearing.

We both turn to find my mother standing a few steps away, her expression a mix of surprise and unmistakable satisfaction. "I thought I might find you two here," she says. "The grapevines are a wonderful place for ... reflection." She smiles and walks away.

We chuckle awkwardly at her not-so-subtle innuendo, but the moment has done its job. Suddenly, Junie and I are more than two people keeping up appearances. We're two people who've shared something genuine.

With the tension of the evening still humming between us, I lead the way to the main building to collect our room key and baggage. The concierge hands it over with a smile, further adding to my internal whirlpool of emotions. I make some casual comment about the architecture of the winery-turned-hotel as a distraction while Junie and I make our way up to our room, our bags rolling quietly behind us.

As I unlock the door and push it open, the first thing that strikes me is how intimate the space is. A king-sized bed with plush white linens takes center stage, framed by tastefully rustic decor—exposed wooden beams on the ceiling and a fireplace built with cobblestones from the vineyard. A pair of wine glasses and a bottle of my cousin's best reserve wine sit on a nearby table, almost as if taunting us with the irony of our situation. The room's ambiance feels more like a honeymoon suite than accommodations for colleagues—or whatever Junie and I are at this point.

She steps in after me, letting out a low whistle as she surveys the room. "Wow, this is ... cozy," she remarks, carefully choosing her words as her gaze lands on the bed. The air in the room is thick with unspoken words and implications. It's as if the universe is urging us to confront the magnetic pull that's been drawing us closer all day.

"I'll, uh, take the couch," I offer, pointing to a small sofa that sits against one wall of the room, knowing it's too narrow to serve as a bed.

Junie shakes her head, her eyes locking onto mine with a mix of amusement and something deeper, something vulnerable. "Let's not kid ourselves. That couch is probably about as comfortable as a bed of nails."

So, we're left with one choice—the king-sized bed that seems both too big and too small for what's transpiring between us. It's the elephant in the room, the stage for a performance neither of us had rehearsed for. And yet, I set down my bag and feel Junie's eyes on me.

"Look, it's not ideal," I say, finally breaking the tension. "But we'll make it work. After all, it's just two nights."

"A wall of pillows is definitely happening." She begins constructing the pillow barrier on the bed, and I'm struck by the convolutedness of it all. Here we are, playing roles yet uncovering truths, both drawn to and wary of whatever this strange connection between us might mean.

For a few seconds, there's silence before we take turns using the bathroom and changing into our pajamas. We take our respective places in bed, Junie on her side of the pillow wall and me on mine.

"Goodnight, AJ," she says, her voice soft and filled with an emotion I can't quite identify.

"Do you want to talk about the kiss?"

"Nope," she says. "I need time to think."

I don't say another word.

As the night grows deeper, and we lie there, a fortress of pillows between us, there's an unsaid understanding. This isn't just about appearances. This isn't just a ruse. There's something real here. But am I ready to face it? She seems lost in thought too, and the room echoes with a silent question—what are we really doing?

CHAPTER FIFTEEN

JUNIE

My eyes flutter open to a cocoon of warmth, and it dawns on me—our pillow wall has crumbled, vanished like morning mist, and I'm draped over AJ's chest like a human blanket. My first instinct is to bolt, to return to my side of the bed before he wakes up. I try to move, but then I feel his chest vibrate slightly as his chuckle fills the air.

His arms cinch around me like a velvet trap. "Planning an escape?"

I shoot him a flustered glance, caught in the act. "Oh, please. As if I'm some sort of cuddle fugitive."

"One who snores like a hibernating bear," he grins, poking my nose with the tip of his finger.

"I do not snore!"

Before I can retreat, his fingers descend, lightning-quick, skimming over my sides. I squirm and laugh, my breaths coming out in tiny, delighted gasps.

His face hovers inches from mine. "Waving the white

flag yet?" Our laughter fades, swallowed by a sudden, electric tension.

His eyes darken. His lips, tantalizingly close, part ever so slightly. The space between us disappears in a magnetic pull. We kiss. No, not just a kiss—a revelation, a thing of passion and promise.

"I can't." I pull away, my voice a whisper laced with regret. "Not while you're—paying me." I shift to sitting and pull the cover up to my chin. "The whole shopping thing was a complete *Pretty Woman* experience, but she was a professional. I'm not. Hell, I can barely score breakfast after a sleepover date."

He exhales softly. "Time to raise your standards."

"I'm trying. That's why I created Love Bug."

"Remember that I don't want you because I'm paying you. I can pay anyone. I want you because I want you. You and I have a connection."

Crickets could throw a concert in the silence that follows. My heart hammers in my chest. Every fiber of me yearns to kiss him again, and yet I can't. "But you're still paying me and until that ends, this can't happen."

"I understand and respect your decision." He changes the subject. "How about some room service?"

"Perfect." I seize the chance to divert. "And while they're assembling our breakfast, I'm hitting the shower." My phone buzzes with a new challenge notification as I enter the bathroom. I glance at it and sigh.

Share your biggest fear.

I wait for the water to heat and get in the shower, letting the hot water sluice over me. The tension still lingers, so palpable it's almost another person in the room. As I lather up, I consider the challenge. My biggest fear is so personal, but isn't that why I designed the app to ask questions of this nature? Getting to the personal parts helps build a relationship. Thinking about that brings me back to AJ's confession—he wants me.

I type, "Alright, you want my deepest, darkest fear? It's ending up alone, okay? Yep, there you have it, navigating this crazy, mixed-up world solo, devoid of the one person who gets all my jokes and doesn't judge me for eating chocolate at 3 a.m., someone who would willingly subject themselves to endless rom-com marathons and be the marshmallow to my hot cocoa, the cheese to my macaroni, the—oh, you get the point!"

I hit send, exhaling like I've just released a part of my soul into the digital void.

Pushing the door open, I step into the room, cloaked in my towel. AJ's eyes, previously lost in his phone, snap up. They roam over me, taking in every curve, every detail.

"You're killing me, Junie," he mutters, his voice a decadent blend of admiration and restraint.

Ah, breakfast. The intoxicating blend of fresh coffee and scrambled eggs wafts through the air, colliding with the lingering notes of my lavender body wash. I grab my robe from the hook behind the door, sliding it over my shoulders as I let the towel tumble to the floor. Now clad in a more morning-appropriate ensemble, we dig in, but the atmosphere is a strange fusion of tension and coziness. The food is delicious, yet AJ's words and my own unresolved feelings buzz between us like a live wire. We eat, but each bite is laced with the unsaid, the undone, the what-might-be.

"Sorry about, you know, invading your territory earlier," I say, setting down my coffee cup with a clatter.

He chuckles, a sound I've come to realize has a comforting timbre, like aged bourbon poured over gravel. "You didn't just cross the line, you erased it. But hey, I'm not filing any complaints."

His words dance through the air, and for a moment, we're lost in each other's eyes—the rich amber of his meeting the forest green of mine. I can almost hear my heart thump in my chest.

Finally, we shake ourselves free of the trance, rising to get dressed. Today's agenda involves attending a wedding, and as AJ commandeers the bathroom, I slide into a tasteful-yet-flirty floral dress. When he opens the door, we exchange places so I can apply my mascara and he can change. Moments later he returns to the bathroom, dressed to kill in a fancy suit and a silk tie he's knotting at his neck. My gaze lingers on his hands, nimble yet strong, and I wonder what it would feel like to have those hands hold me close—without any barriers, physical or otherwise.

After slicking on my lip gloss, I declare myself complete and fully attired, and we exit the room. The clack of my heels on the polished hallway melds with the heavier footsteps of AJ's dress shoes. As we descend in the elevator, I can feel the anticipation building, a rising crescendo of emotions and desires. The surrounding air is thickening with what could be, what should be, what—despite all odds—might just be.

As we arrive at the wedding venue set amidst the grape vines, the air is already charged with the electricity of impending vows. Flower-laden arches create a natural aisle, and sunlight filters through grape leaves, casting dappled patterns on the guests. The fragrance of blooming roses mingles with the fruity scent of ripe grapes. As the ceremony unfolds, my senses sharpen. I become acutely aware of the whisper of silk and satin as the bride moves, the harmonious chords of a string quartet providing the soundtrack to this romantic tableau, and the bride's laughter sounding like a song in the gentle breeze. The ceremony ends as quickly as it begins, leading to more festivities.

In the soft glow of the hanging lanterns, with the rhythm of the music pulling me in, I can't help but feel at ease. Gone is the Junie who would have second-guessed her every step, wondering if she looked out of place. Now, there's just the thrill of the moment and the man I'm with. The world fades away, and it's just AJ and me in a sea of swirling colors and joyous laughter.

Sophia, in her meticulous designer gown, stands to one side, sipping her champagne gracefully. Our eyes meet for a brief second, her gaze assessing and judging. She represents everything I thought I needed to be—polished, refined, and always in control. But AJ's hand on my waist, his smile genuine and filled with mischief, reminds me that maybe being imperfect is what makes life interesting.

He leans down to whisper, "You light up this place, Junie." His words surprise me, but his eyes give away no lies. As we continue to move with the beat, I spot Sophia again, talking to a group. Yet, in her poised perfection, there's an undeniable air of predictability.

AJ seems to follow my gaze, and his lips twitch into a smirk. "I once thought that's what I wanted, you know?

"And now?" I ask as he spins me around.

He pulls me closer, his eyes searching mine. "Now?" he echoes, letting the word hang between us for a tantalizing moment. "Let's just say I'm more confused than I've ever been." With that, he dips me low, leaving my heart racing and mind swirling with questions.

This morning, I set all the rules and boundaries. He was pushing forward, and I pushed him back. I haven't made it easy. The lines between real and pretend are blurring, but we need to see this through to discover what lies beyond.

Next is the bouquet toss, that age-old harbinger of nuptial fate. A collective giggle rises from the crowd, a blend of anticipation and playful competition. Almost on autopilot, I find myself amid a group of hopefuls. The bride spins and releases the bouquet into the air. Time slows, and I reach up. My fingers grasp soft petals—I've caught it.

Applause erupts, but AJ's voice rises above it, proud and clear. "That's my girl!" Our eyes lock, but I know it's just make-believe.

The wedding celebrations wind down, the air still buzzing with the hum of conversation and laughter. AJ and I say our farewells to everyone, and as we return to our room, the gravel crunches beneath our feet, each step echoing my emotional churn. It was all so real for being fake.

His phone rings, and he excuses himself as I return to the room alone. I step back inside, and a wave of conflicting emotions washes over me. I need to talk to someone, and grab my phone to dial Liv.

"Hey Liv, you free?" I ask as soon as she picks up.

"Always. How's the wedding? How's AJ?"

"You wouldn't believe it even if I told you," I sigh, pacing across the plush hotel carpet, its fibers tickling my toes with each step. "Caught the bouquet, Liv. I was like a wide receiver in the Super Bowl of love, or at least that's what it felt like."

There's a pause, and Liv says, "So, what does that mean to you?"

"It feels like catching that bouquet wasn't just about snagging some flowers, you know? It's like I caught feelings, too. Big, gnarly, bewildering feelings."

As I talk, my eyes catch my reflection in the room's full-length mirror. I see a woman grappling with her emotions, trying to sort out her tangled heart.

"I get you," Liv's voice softens, understanding washing over her words. "Feelings are complicated, messy even. You've got to figure yours out, okay?"

I lean against the wall, its cool surface contrasting sharply with the warmth flooding my cheeks. "It's like I'm standing on the edge of this beautiful, terrifying cliff. I could take the leap, feel the exhilarating rush, but I could also, you know, end up in a heap of emotional wreckage."

"Love is a leap, Junie," she says. "Always has been, always will be. You'll never know unless you jump. But listen, if AJ's the one you're considering this leap with, you'd better be sure he's also willing to jump with you."

As if on cue, the door swings open, and AJ strides in, his phone call concluded. He looks almost otherworldly. My heart beats an erratic rhythm as if mimicking the chaotic dance of my thoughts.

"So, what's your next move, Junie?" Liv asks, her voice lingering in my ear as I lock eyes with AJ.

The air thickens between us, charged and expectant, as if the universe is holding its breath for my next decision.

"I'll let you know," I say and hang up.

AJ holds an expression I can't quite decode—something between yearning and respectful distance. He looks every bit the leading man of a romance yet to be fully written.

His eyes travel down to the bouquet, still clutched in my hands like some emotional lifeline. "Looks like you've caught more than just a bunch of flowers, huh?"

The words hang between us, rich with subtext. It's like a complex wine. I can almost taste the layers—hints of vulnerability, overtones of desire, undertones of emotional risk.

"Yeah," I finally say, setting the bouquet down on the table as if distancing myself from its symbolic weight could simplify the intricate tapestry of feelings that has ensnared me. "Looks like it."

My phone, still in my hand, feels like an intruder in this intimate space. Liv's question echoes in my head. *What will you do now, Junie?*

AJ moves closer, and I catch the scent of his cologne. It reaches into me and stirs something primal.

"Junie, I—"

Before he can complete the sentence, my phone buzzes again. A message from the dating app.

Challenge completed. Next challenge— What's your biggest dream for love?

A sigh escapes me, a blend of irritation and relief. Here, encapsulated in this message, is the next step, yet another question demanding an answer I'm not sure I'm ready to give.

"Who's it from?" AJ asks, his voice touched with curiosity, maybe even a hint of jealousy.

"Just Liv asking questions I don't have answers to," I reply, chuckling but feeling every unsaid word between us.

And so, we stand there, on the edge of something new, something thrilling, something terrifying. Liv's question still hovers, unanswered, yet more pressing than ever. What will I do now?

With my phone silenced and set aside, the atmosphere shifts once again. The emotional terrain we navigate is as complex as the lush vineyards outside— verdant and full of potential, yet fraught with uncertainties. My senses are heightened, each one attuned to AJ's presence. From the resonance of his voice to the enticing aroma of his cologne, it's as if my body and soul are conspiring to push me closer to him.

"Junie," he begins, his voice steeped in an emotion that quickens my pulse, "I know things are complicated. I know there's a lot we need to sort through. But it's hard to deny that something real is happening here. Don't you feel it?"

His eyes lock onto mine, and for a breathless second, all my defenses waver. I feel it in every stolen glance, accidental touch, and lingering moment of silence filled only by the pounding of my heart.

"I do," I admit, the words coming out in a whisper. "I feel it, too."

He takes a step closer, each footfall a question mark. "What are we going to do about it?"

Before I have a chance to answer, my phone buzzes. It's Liv, as if she's sensed the critical juncture and needs to weigh in. Her timing, impeccable as always, adds yet another layer to an already convoluted situation.

AJ's expression changes, a hint of a smirk lighting up his features. "Are you going to get that?"

I gaze at the phone and then back at him. "No," I say. "Some questions need answering, but this one—what we're going to do—can't wait any longer."

His eyes meet mine, and I see a kaleidoscope of emotions—hope, fear, desire, doubt. Yet, above all, there's a silent understanding that we're both on the edge of something life-changing, something neither of us can fully articulate but sincerely want to explore.

And so, Liv's call, muted and unanswered, fades into the background, leaving AJ's question lingering in the air, filling the room, my thoughts, and my soul. What are we going to do about it?

CHAPTER SIXTEEN

AJ

As I lock eyes with Junie, the air between us sizzles, each second stretching into a tantalizing eternity. Her lips part, a silent invitation. A rush of warmth floods my cheeks. We're on the precipice of something amazing. Just a sliver of distance, a shared breath away from crossing that line, and—

A loud knock sounds at the door. I move to open it, and my mother walks in, a whirlwind of Chanel No. 5 and unyielding determination.

"Darlings, look what I've brought!" Her eyes sparkle with an intoxicating blend of mischief and delight, but I notice the tightness around her smile, the telltale sign that she's up to something. My gut churns—part relief, part disappointment, a paradox of gratitude and regret. Mom's entrance is like a wrecking ball to our moment, leaving behind a rubble of unsaid words and unfulfilled desires.

Mixed emotions surge through me. A reluctant sigh

of relief escapes me, as if dodging a bullet I'm not sure I wanted to avoid.

Mom parades in with Junie's forgotten purse dangling from her arm, three champagne flutes hanging from her fingers like ornaments, and a bottle of champagne cradled like a newborn. "Ah, Junie, you left this at the wedding," Mom says, dangling the purse like a lure. "And I thought, why not toast to love? Especially since you caught the bouquet."

She plops the champagne bottle on the coffee table, its label flaunting cursive promises of vintage elegance. Then she pries the cork out. A jubilant pop resounds, and she pours the effervescent liquid into crystal flutes with a chemist's precision. "Since you're obviously next in line to get hitched," she beams at Junie, "there's no time like the present to start planning your dream wedding."

Junie's eyes widen, her brows leaping toward her hairline as if they want to escape the room. I glance at her, and our eyes lock in a silent conversation only we can understand. A cascade of emotions rushes over her features—panic, disbelief, and a twinge of curiosity. She's a book whose pages I've skimmed but never deeply read, yet in this moment, the message is crystal clear. This isn't where we are headed.

"Mom," I start, rubbing the back of my neck, "we were just—"

"Hanging out," Junie chimes in, finishing my sentence as she clutches her purse like a life preserver.

"We don't get to spend this kind of time with each other, so we're using it to get to know each other better."

"That's the thing about love," Mom interjects, swirling her champagne. "You never really know one another until you're sharing a closet and arguing about which way the toilet paper should hang."

The atmosphere thickens with awkwardness, a viscous soup of what-ifs and not-yets, stirred by my mother's indomitable enthusiasm. "Mom, hold on," I say, my eyes tracing the delicate bubbles rising in the champagne flute. "Junie and I, we're not ... we're not at a point where we're discussing weddings."

"Exactly," Junie adds, her voice a little shaky, as if she's walking a tightrope of diplomacy. "We're just enjoying our time together, taking things slow."

Mom's eyes narrow momentarily, her perceptive gaze cutting through our words. "Oh, come now! I saw you two kiss last night. That wasn't just a peck on the cheek. You can't fake that kind of passion." She sips her champagne as if she laid down a winning hand in a high-stakes poker game.

"And besides," she adds with a wink, "the universal truth is that eggs are fresher before your thirties. Yours are nearing their expiration date. Why wait when love is in the air?"

The room fills with a palpable tension. Junie's eyes flit to me, and I can see her mentally grappling with my mother's words. She's not wrong. That kiss was electric, like touching a live wire. But turning a spark into a full-blown fire? That's a different beast altogether. Then there's the comment about Junie's prime fertility.

Junie raises an eyebrow, her lips curling into a playful smile. "Oh, don't worry about me being in my prime. I just read about a 59-year-old woman who gave birth. So, I'd say my biological clock has plenty of ticks left."

AJ's mother bursts into laughter and takes a seat in a nearby chair. "Well, that's one way to look at it. But just imagine needing a walker to attend your child's high school graduation."

Junie winks. "At least I'll never lose my seat. I'll just plop down wherever I am."

"As lovely as your observations are, Mom," I say, hoping humor will be the salve for this uncomfortable situation, "love isn't something to rush. Especially not with someone as special as Junie."

Mom cocks an eyebrow, clearly not ready to relinquish her point. "Special enough for a passionate kiss but not a lifetime commitment?"

Her words linger in the air, a challenge covered in the sweet scent of vintage champagne. It's as if she's thrown down the gauntlet, urging us to pick it up or step away.

"Mom, it's not that simple," I say, my voice tinged with frustration and disbelief. "One passionate moment doesn't equate to forever."

"Yeah," Junie joins in, her voice reinforcing my own. "A kiss is a kiss. It doesn't mean we're ready for beach or castle wedding venue decisions."

My mother chuckles, clearly amused, as she leans

back into the plush cushion. "Oh, a beach or a castle, is it? How about this—band or DJ?"

"Mom, you're getting ahead of yourself," I say, my eyes rolling even as a reluctant smile tugs at my lips. "Junie and I are nowhere near planning a wedding. We don't know if we're ready to plan our next date."

Mom's eyes soften, and for a moment, her relentless enthusiasm gives way to genuine concern. "Well, all right then. But if you two decide to jump off this romantic cliff together someday, just know that the parachute of family support will be ready and waiting." She raises her champagne flute in a mock toast and downs the remaining bubbles in one swift gulp.

Junie and I share a lingering look, both of us silently processing my mother's whirlwind visit and what it means for whatever "this" is between us.

"Before you burst in, Mom, we were just getting ready to practice," I say, my voice dripping with irony.

Mom's eyes light up, catching the innuendo immediately. "Oh, well then, practice makes perfect, doesn't it?" She chuckles, rises, and heads for the door. "You two better get back to your, ahem, rehearsals."

Mom exits with a wink and a flourish, closing the door behind her. As soon as I hear the latch click, the room expands, and the atmosphere changes instantaneously. Junie and I exchange a look, a potent blend of relief, yearning, and awkwardness. My eyes meet hers, and for a moment, we're both frozen, caught in the whirlpool of emotions.

"I can't stay in this room, on that bed, and not do

what we're both thinking," I say, my voice hoarse with suppressed longing. My eyes drop to the enticing softness of the mattress, the plush pillows, and the sheets— unspoiled territory that now screams with temptation.

Junie's gaze follows mine, her eyes clouding with a similar look. "Yeah, you're right," she finally says, her voice tinged with regret and relief.

My eyes flit to the suitcases in the corner, a visual metaphor for our emotional baggage. "We've got five minutes to pack, Junie. Otherwise, we're crossing a bridge we can't walk back from."

My words hang in the air. For a moment, Junie's lips part as if she's about to say something, her eyes filled with a complex mixture of emotions. But instead, she nods, silently acknowledging the precarious tightrope we find ourselves balancing on.

As she fills her suitcase, the zipper punctuates the air, underscoring the tension between intimacy and separation. I toss my clothes haphazardly in my bag and wait by the door.

Finally, her eyes meet mine again, and I see an array of emotions—doubt, desire, and an indecipherable blend of hope and caution. "Ready," she says softly, her voice laden with vulnerability.

"Let's go," I reply, equally soft, looking around the room that could have been the birthplace of something beautiful and problematic. A lingering question haunts me. Would diving into this uncharted territory be a mistake we'd regret, or would the real regret be never taking the plunge?

CHAPTER SEVENTEEN

JUNIE

The car's interior cradles me in a cocoon of soft leather, while the air carries AJ's signature scent—a blend of clean masculinity that's become as familiar as my own. My eyes fixate on how his hands grip the steering wheel—confident but not overbearing, as if he's struck a harmonious balance between assertion and gentleness. I wonder what those same hands would be like on my body.

Would his fingers race across my skin, chasing immediate satisfaction like a car gunning through a yellow light? Or would they be slow, deliberate—each touch a calculated stroke, as if he's charting a new geographic discovery? I can almost feel the phantom sensation of his fingertips tracing intricate patterns across my skin, each point of contact lingering like a cartographer's ink on an unfinished map.

My mind drifts, and I replay scenarios that have never unfolded. Us, together, in a space where time loses meaning, where every sigh and shiver reveals another layer of a complex, evolving landscape.

Would he be the kind to rush toward the final destination, or would he revel in the journey itself? I'm torn between the two possibilities, each loaded with its own set of expectations and disappointments. The thrill of urgency has its appeal. It speaks to raw need, to uncontainable desire. But then there's the allure of slowness, a meandering exploration that leaves no stone unturned, where every minute elongates, filling with the kind of details that turn mundane experiences into cherished memories.

And then, there's me—caught in this web of hypotheticals, clinging to what could have been. The what-ifs pool in my chest, a murky well of longing and indecision, each question a droplet that adds to an already brimming reservoir.

As I glimpse at AJ, his attention riveted on the winding road ahead, he remains unaware of the emotional exploration happening just inches away. I can't help but question, do I claim even a tiny territory in the map of his thoughts?

As we pull up to the curb of my apartment, the tension inside the car merges as if we're both teetering on the edge, hesitant to make the next move. AJ shifts the car into park, and the engine goes quiet, leaving us in a momentary stillness that magnifies every thought between us.

AJ exits the car with a composed demeanor that

shows nothing of what he's thinking. I watch through the passenger window as he rounds the vehicle to come to my side. The car door swings open, and I'm met with a gentle look in his eyes—a look that simultaneously holds possibilities and hesitations.

He offers me his hand, and as I grasp it to step out, the physical touch sends a jolt through me, accentuating my hunger for a different kind of connection—one sealed with a kiss. The question taunts me. Will he lean in? I want that kiss. There's no doubt about that. Yet the implication bears down on me like an invisible force.

A kiss would mean reopening the intricate maze of emotions we left unresolved at the winery.

"I hope you had a good time," he says softly, letting go of my hand.

"Yes," I respond, my voice filled with sincerity, "I did."

We lock eyes, and for a heartbeat, it feels like the world holds its breath, waiting for one of us to make a move—to break the stalemate. But then his gaze shifts away, landing somewhere over my shoulder. It's as if he, too, realizes that a kiss could undo both of us, throwing us back into an emotional tangle neither of us is ready to unravel.

"Good night, Junie." The words hang in the air, marked with finality.

As I stand on my doorstep, I turn to find AJ already fishing something out of his back pocket. His hand surfaces, clutching an envelope. "For your expenses," he says, offering it like a peace treaty.

My fingers close around the envelope, and instantly, an uneasy sensation grips me, like I've just accepted something that's far heavier than the paper the money is printed on. I try to wrestle my thoughts into clarity, and a bizarre image floats into my mind—I see myself as an escort. Not the kind in lurid tales or seedy motels, but more like arm candy, someone who shows up, glitters for a while under the spotlight and is then paid for the effort. *But why does it have to feel this way?* I grapple with the conflicting emotions swirling within me. I never signed up to be someone's showpiece. The money was for living expenses, a simple, practical arrangement we'd agreed upon. No strings attached, or so I thought.

Yet, here I am, my stomach churning as if I've swallowed something that refuses to settle. A snicker escapes my lips, the irony not lost on me. What an intricate web I find myself caught in, trying to pin down my feelings about an envelope stuffed with cash while wrestling with far more complicated sentiments for the man who gave it to me.

I quickly smile at AJ. "Thank you." He nods and walks away.

As I unlock my door, I remind myself that it's just a few weeks until the competition ends. The words are a mantra, repeated to strip the moment of its loaded implications. But even as I step into my apartment, envelope in hand, the money feels heavy—a piece of evidence marking the boundary of our relationship, delineating what could and could not be.

I shut the door behind me, leaning against it momentarily as if its solid presence could stabilize my swirling emotions. The room is dark, filled with the muted shades of streetlights filtering through the curtains. I press my hand to my lips, futilely attempting to capture a kiss that never happened.

With a sigh, I move deeper into my apartment, dropping my suitcase in the corner, and shedding my shoes and dress as if they're layers of a persona I no longer wish to wear. The emptiness here feels amplified tonight, echoing the hollow space within me. My fingers graze the futon, lingering momentarily before I sink into its cushions, surrendering to my thoughts.

In the stillness, my mind replays the weekend, each moment unfurling like a film reel. The laughter we shared, the glances we exchanged, and those silent intervals filled with a tension that hummed like an electric current. And then the finale—a closed car door, a brief exchange of money, and a void where a simple kiss should have been.

The apartment is silent, except for the soft ticking of the wall clock, each tick another reminder of opportunities lost. My eyes wander to the photographs that line my shelves, frozen snippets of happy times spent with family and friends, and I wonder if AJ and I will ever share a captured moment framed and displayed with sentimental value.

I clutch a throw pillow, hugging it to my chest as if it can absorb the jumble of feelings roiling within me—frustration, yearning, and a smidgen of relief. Maybe AJ's absence of action had been a form of protection, a boundary drawn to keep us from straying into emotional territory fraught with complications.

But that thought only comforts me for so long. The clock continues its inexorable march, time slipping through my fingers like grains of sand, and I'm left to wrestle with this new sense of longing—an aching need for something that remains out of reach.

As I sit there, cushioning my thoughts with the soft embrace of the pillow, my phone sits on the coffee table—a silent beacon calling out to me. Recalling Liv's last text takes little effort, her inquisitive words a nudge, always encouraging me to open up and share. The screen seems to beckon, offering an outlet, a friend at the ready to soak up my unfurling narrative.

Yet, my hand hovers, suspended in hesitation. I unlock the phone and open our message thread, my thumb lingering above the virtual keyboard. I could type it all out, every nuanced emotion, every silent wish. But the truth sets in. What would I say that's new? The story remains the same—a weekend saturated in feelings yet lacking any actual conclusion.

I feel coiled, like a spring tightened to its limit, holding potential energy but no release in sight. An internal dialogue battles within me. *Do I burden Liv with my feelings when nothing has shifted? When all I have are questions on top of more questions?*

Choosing not to navigate that conversational maze, I lock the phone and place it back on the table. It's not that

I don't want Liv's support, but expressing these thoughts might solidify them into a reality I'm not ready to accept.

So, I sit, dwelling in my self-constructed sanctuary of silence, hugging the uncertainty to my chest. There's comfort in not having to dissect each emotion, in leaving some things unresolved. But as I close my eyes, even that small comfort can't silence the persistent whispers of what might have been, now echoing louder in the chambers of my mind.

My eyelids flutter open at the sudden buzz from my phone, the screen's glow piercing the room's dim atmosphere. A notification pops up, lighting my face with its message.

New secrets revealed. Find out your match's deepest confessions.

My heart skips a beat. It's from my dating app, and I'd almost forgotten about it in this AJ-induced emotional whirlpool.

A wave of curiosity overtakes me. Each revealed secret is like a gift. Tapping the notification, I navigate to the app.

I often overanalyze situations. I wish I could be more spontaneous.

The words hover on the screen, each letter imbued with a mystery that beckons for closer examination.

For a heartbeat, I consider the possibility. Could this be AJ? I shake my head. No, it can't be. The man I know exudes decisiveness, a self-assurance that almost borders on arrogance. Still, the confession lingers in my mind like a puzzle demanding to be solved.

As I sit back, my thoughts swirl around the many facets of AJ I've come to know—the man of action, the unyielding competitor, and the vulnerable soul hiding behind layers of self-constructed armor. Would such a man wish for spontaneity? Or is it more likely that this confession belongs to someone else?

The words continue to hover in my thoughts, each letter etching deeper into my consciousness. "Often over-analyzes situations, wishes to be more spontaneous." I shake my head, dismissing the notion almost as quickly as it arises. AJ, the man who orchestrates every detail of his life down to the last second? That doesn't align with the portrait I've painted of him in my mind.

And yet, a sliver of doubt remains, a thread weaving itself through the fabric of my convictions. I remember the wine tasting, his expression contemplative as he swirled the glass but decisive when choosing the perfect vintage.

Even more confusing is the recollection of his words, a memory from a conversation that now feels like ages ago. We discussed the characters from *Pretty in Pink*, a world apart in social status, facing the insurmountable wall of "what will people think?" He'd said it would never work out, that they were too different. Yet the sentiment behind his voice felt personal as if he were talking about us—him and me, Junie, and AJ, two souls from different spheres colliding.

I clutch my phone tighter as if squeezing it can force

the truth out of those tiny pixels. Should I explore other possibilities? Should I focus on a future that doesn't involve AJ?

I exhale, my breath shaky, as if releasing the uncertainty that has encapsulated me. Perhaps I've been approaching this all wrong. Maybe it's time to shift the focus from pondering AJ's hidden depths to considering what I genuinely want and what's realistically achievable. After all, if I keep reaching for pie-in-the-sky dreams, I might miss the possibilities spread before me.

As the room settles back into its familiar quiet, a new clarity dawns on me. I reflect on the day's events, dissecting each moment and weighing it against my escalating emotions. And in that silent contemplation, an unsettling realization emerges—perhaps AJ's decisive nature had been a net cast just in time to catch us both from tumbling into the unknown.

His quick decision to withdraw, to abstain from a parting kiss, suddenly takes on a new meaning. I begin to appreciate the strength it must have taken to pump the brakes when it seemed like we were on the verge of crossing an irrevocable line. That decision, a manifestation of his analytical mind, might have spared us both from complications neither of us is prepared for.

I rise from the futon, cover my shoulders in my chunky cable knit throw, and step toward the window. The city outside is alive, each glowing window a small universe teeming with its own stories, secrets, and unresolved tensions. Among these countless narratives, ours is a chapter, not destined to be a book.

For the first time since meeting AJ, I feel a sense of relief wash over me. Relief that our story didn't take a perilous turn, that we've been granted more time to figure things out—or not. Either way, the relief is mixed with gratitude, an unspoken thank you to AJ for his untimely wisdom, for making a choice that, in the end, might have been the most loving thing he could do.

And so, with this newfound perspective, I feel lighter. The room no longer feels oppressive but instead radiates a muted promise, as if whispering that it's okay not to have all the answers, that sometimes the most courageous thing to do is to let things be.

Just when I think I've settled into a newfound serenity, my phone buzzes. The screen lights up, and the dating app is again announcing an opportunity.

Field trip seeking love? Take a ferry to Alcatraz tomorrow at 10:00 to release your imprisoned heart and meet your happily ever after. Reservations are in your name if you choose to take a chance on love.

I chuckle, a disbelieving laugh that floats through the room. Alcatraz—infamous island prison, a fortress of seclusion, and now ... a romantic getaway? It's almost laughable. Yet, my mind stirs, pondering the metaphorical implications. Could Alcatraz, a place once designed to keep people away, be where love finds its freedom?

As my thumb hovers over the "Accept" button, my thoughts flit to AJ. He'd probably scoff at such a whimsical notion, dismissing it as a tourist trap devoid of real emotional merit. Yet, a part of me wonders what he'd really think.

With a press of a button, I accept the field trip invitation. A sense of adventure flares within me, a small spark eager to be fanned into flame.

My finger lingers on the screen, the confirmation message glowing back at me.

Field trip to Alcatraz: Confirmed.

I know once I arrive, the app will lead me to my destiny. If it says I'll meet my happily ever after, it will probably drop the ladybug avatar and show me my soul mate.

A myriad of emotions swirls within, from exhilaration to apprehension, but overriding them all is a sense of anticipation. Maybe love, or at least the possibility of it, is hiding in the least expected places, waiting for people like me to discover it.

I set the phone down, its mission accomplished for the evening. Today, the winding path that is my love life has forked, and I've chosen a direction. It's a small step but a giant leap for me personally. Because today, I've chosen not to be defined by what could have been with AJ or anyone else. Today, I've decided to explore, open myself to new horizons, and listen closely to my heart's murmurings.

As I prepare for bed, a sense of peace envelops me, akin to the quiet that follows a storm. Tomorrow, I'll embark on this unusual journey to Alcatraz, unsure of what I'll find. But one thing is clear—I'm willing to look, to seek, and perhaps to discover love in places as unlikely as a former island prison.

In that willingness, I find my courage. And so, as I slip under the covers, my last thought before drifting into slumber is one of eager anticipation for the unknown.

CHAPTER EIGHTEEN

AJ

The car's engine hums. It's almost like background noise in a busy office, easily drowned out by the thoughts spiraling through my head. My fingers grip the steering wheel, its leather cool and comforting to the touch as I navigate the evening roads. Streetlights cast a glow, a fusion of oranges, purples, and blues painting the sky, yet its beauty barely registers in my preoccupied mind. Each thought I have weaves another intricate thread in a web of curiosity and captivation, all spun around one person—Junie.

The weekend with her lingers in my senses like a vivid, captivating presentation, the kind that leaves you pondering long after the conference room lights go back up. What is it about her? She's engaging, complicated, fascinating, and infuriating all at once. She challenges my analytical mindset in a way no spreadsheet or data analysis ever could. Every time I think I've figured her out, she turns, shifts, and I'm back to square one. She's a Rubik's cube, and I've lost the cheat sheet.

As I turn up the volume on the radio, a haunting guitar riff from a classic 80s rock ballad fills the car, offering a temporary distraction. But even the music can't drown out the nagging theory forming in my mind. Could Junie be the enigma behind the app? The timing, the intellectual and emotional rapport, the electricity between us—it's as if all the variables align, suggesting a conclusion too compelling to ignore.

I find myself mulling over the app, which is supposed to reveal its match soon. Could Junie be behind this, rigging the system to pair us? Nah, she doesn't seem the scheming type. But then again, there's a lot of money at stake here. Enough to cloud anyone's judgment.

The stretch of road ahead unfolds like the limitless possibilities of a new fiscal year, which is to say, both exciting and terrifying. I inhale deeply, filling my lungs with the scent of the new car air freshener—pleasant but a poor stand-in for Junie's blend of jasmine and uncharted territories.

As the miles stretch behind me, my mind keeps circling back to Junie. In her life's ledger, am I just another financial entry, or could I be the bedrock investment she's been searching for?

The thought worms its way into my conscience, unsettling yet inviting. Do I even want to be just another high-value asset in the grand balance sheet of Junie's life? My role in previous relationships has been a secure investment offering stability and growth. But what the app offers, what Junie potentially offers, teases the imagination with the idea of more.

More—a word so simple yet brimming with possibility. It suggests a symbiotic partnership, not just an addition to a portfolio. It hints at late-night talks, lazy morning kisses, shared laughter, and mutual dreams. More than numbers on a screen, more than a social or financial capital boost.

The world outside momentarily pauses as I pull up to a red stoplight. It's one of those long ones that gives you too much time to think, or enough time to question all your life choices. My phone buzzes, a subtle vibration against the console. Picking it up, I see a notification from the app.

New insight: Your match's deepest fear revealed.

I tap the message, and my eyes move across the screen.

Alright, you want my deepest, darkest fear? It's ending up alone, okay? Yep, there you have it, navigating this crazy, mixed-up world solo, devoid of the one person who gets all my quirky jokes and doesn't judge me for eating chocolate at 3 a.m., someone who would willingly subject themselves to endless rom-com marathons and be the marshmallow to my hot cocoa, the cheese to my macaroni, the—oh, you get the point!

The words echo in the silent cabin, a reverberation

bouncing back and forth in the limited space, hitting me square in the chest. The voice in the text, the tone—it's unmistakably her, or at least it could be. It's as if Junie's soul has leaped from the screen, jumbled up in words and fears that sound so distinctly her. And yet, doubt creeps in. What if it's not her?

The idea of being alone forever, articulated with such vividness, strikes a chord. It's as though someone ripped a page from my own journal of insecurities and fears and threw it back at me as an app notification.

I accelerate as the light turns green, but my thoughts remain stuck at that intersection. My grip tightens around the wheel, and I swallow, my throat suddenly parched. The car moves forward, but those words drag behind.

A voice in my mind whispers, *But what if it is her? And what if this fear, this vividly painted dread of solitude, is the common thread that binds us together?*

The car engine falls silent as I pull into my parking spot. I pluck my phone from the console as it buzzes—a new challenge from the app.

Field trip seeking love? Take a ferry to Alcatraz tomorrow at 10:00 to release your imprisoned heart and meet your happily ever after. Reservations are in your name if you choose to take a chance on love.

Alcatraz. A shiver courses through me. The place is a stark symbol of isolation, a fortress of solitude. It's the antithesis of what one seeks in love, yet it mirrors my trepidation about it. Love has often felt like a prison to me—an emotional lockdown where vulnerabilities are exposed, with no guarantee of parole.

I exit the car. Before entering the building, I pause, while my finger hovers over the "Accept" button on the app's challenge. A frisson of dread and excitement moves within me. What am I doing? I tap it. No turning back now.

Once inside, I take the elevator past my offices to the penthouse where I live. The door shuts behind me with a decisive click, sealing me in my sanctuary. I'm reminded of the contrast between these empty rooms and the vibrant, messy, emotional landscape that Junie represents. If she's there tomorrow, I could end my self-imposed emotional incarceration.

I undress and get ready for bed. Lying in the soft sheets, the night presses against my window like a dark, implied promise. Junie invades my thoughts. Her laughter echoes in my mind, reverberating like a ripple through a still pond.

As sleep claims me, I can't help but wonder what the dawn will bring.

MORNING CRACKS its way into my room, rays of sunlight streaking through the blinds and pulling me from my slumber. I reach for my phone, squinting against its harsh light, and dial Henry.

"Hey, Henry. Listen, I won't be in today. You're

running the show," I inform him, voice still tinged with sleep.

"Taking a personal day, eh?" Henry responds, chuckling on the other end. "What's the occasion?"

"Seeking parole from the prison of my life. Think *Shawshank*, but less mud and more introspection."

Henry roars with laughter. "Ah, the ever-elusive quest for freedom. Well, good luck with your jailbreak, Andy Dufresne."

As I hang up, a smile etches its way onto my face. If Junie shows up today, it's more than just a get-out-of-jail-free card. I have to believe that the app, with its complicated algorithms, knows what it's doing and that this crazy urge to strip her naked and make love goes way deeper than physical attraction. She promised a connection, and despite my reservations, I'm increasingly convinced she could be right.

Still holding the phone, I navigate to Junie's contact and tap out a quick message.

So, what's on your agenda today?

The moments waiting for her reply stretch out, each tick of the clock amplifying the drumming of my own heartbeat. Finally, the screen lights up.

Exploring the mysteries of breakfast cereals and contemplating my existence. How about you?

A smile unfurls on my lips. Junie is always disguising her answers with humor. But is she hinting at something deeper? If she's going to Alcatraz, would she be upfront about it?

Sinking back onto the bed, I am entranced by the animated ellipsis that signals her continuing to type. What else is she adding? More jokes or a nugget of truth, perhaps?

Impulsively, my fingers tap out a response.

Got an interesting day lined up. Catch you later?

As long as my cereal research doesn't take all day, she types back.

How can something that tastes so good be so awful for you?

I lay the phone beside me and lock my eyes onto the ceiling. Her response, funny yet enigmatic, neither confirms nor denies.

Suddenly, the full scope of the day hits me. If Junie appears at Alcatraz, some invisible hand—fate, the app, or blind luck—has intervened in our lives. But if she's absent, what then? Do I re-evaluate and start my calculations anew without her as a variable?

These questions buzz in my head like a swarm of bees, each stinging. I rise from the bed, setting my jaw. The day stretches before me, laden with possibility. Time to meet it head-on.

I walk over to my desk, my eyes scanning the array of tasks and projects neatly lined up—each one a cog in the complex machinery of my professional life. But today, the stakes are personal. Today's gamble doesn't involve market shares or quarterly reports. It's an investment in my happiness, something I haven't financed in a long time.

I find my reservation on the Alcatraz ferry site, pay for it, and print it. It's surprisingly heavy for such a small piece of paper. I contemplate it as I would a shareholder contract, with each clause and term a binding commitment. Going means confronting the possibilities I've entertained in my most private moments. It means being vulnerable, a state I often equate with emotional bankruptcy.

I decide then, a resolute nod as if sealing a deal. I'm going to Alcatraz. If Junie is there, the payoff could be life-altering. And if she isn't, well, at least I've done due diligence in exploring this venture of the heart.

As I don casual clothes, each piece adds a layer of authenticity, like updating my personal profile after years of neglect.

Keys, phone, and ferry ticket in hand, I hesitate at the door. Today isn't about dodging or finding loopholes in love. It's about market research in my life's least-explored sector—my feelings and desires.

I step out, locking the door behind me, and work my way to the parking garage and my car. The drive is short, and I exit the car, locking it behind me as I approach the bustling ferry terminal. The atmosphere here feels like a stock exchange for human emotions—couples, families, and lone adventurers all buying tickets to different experiences.

My eyes briefly scan the crowd. Could she be here? The thought hammers at the back of my mind.

I retrieve my ticket from my pocket, turning it over in my hands. I line up and wait.

As the boat looms larger, so does the gravity of my decision to come here today. I climb aboard, taking a seat near the rail. The engine rumbles, and the ferry begins its journey across the water. Every churning wave the boat slices through seems to resonate with my internal turbulence. Yet, amidst the chaos, a thought crystallizes—this is my choice, my venture. Regardless of today's outcome, I'm steering this ship, not my mother.

I clutch the rail as the boat pulls into the dock. Then, it hits me. Alcatraz looms ahead, an unforgiving island that has served as a fortress and a prison. Today, it has become the arena where my most-guarded hopes and fears will be reckoned with.

As I leave the ferry and step onto the island, the air is filled with brine and rust, each scent leaving its imprint on me as I wander through Alcatraz's pathways.

I look to every nook, cranny, and doorway that might conceal a hidden figure. Each red-haired woman I glimpse quickens my pulse and triggers a burst of adrenaline. Could it be her? Is Junie here?

Walking past the looming guard towers and dilapidated cells, the island's history surrounds me like an iron shackle. These confining walls, once designed to contain, now serve as a means to set me free.

I press on, passing through the library, the cafeteria, and rooms where human stories unfolded in layers, much like the scenarios playing out in my mind. Despite this, I find no trace of Junie. She's not tucked away in a corner reading a book, not among the crowds listening to a guide's spiel, not capturing the moment in a selfie against the backdrop of a decaying cell block.

Each vacant space where I hope to find her presence amplifies my isolation and loneliness. I am on an island, surrounded by water and walls, yet it's as if the walls of my own making are holding me captive.

CHAPTER NINETEEN

JUNIE

In front of my closet, the morning light gently highlights my colorful clothes. Today is no ordinary day—it could be the day I finally meet "the one," thanks to Love Bug. How does one even dress for such an occasion?

Finally, my eyes settle on a graphic T-shirt that screams "Junie" in every possible way. Adorned with the words "Whale You Be Mine?" and featuring an endearing cartoon whale, it epitomizes my quirky charm. Laughing softly to myself, I slip the shirt over my head.

It's both funny and sassy, and if Mr. Right is out there, he'll need to appreciate my unique sense of humor. Paired with my go-to jeans and Vans Convict sneakers, I'm a love warrior ready for whatever Alcatraz throws me. A tingling sensation of excitement courses through me as I snatch up my bag and bolt out the door, prepared to discover what destiny has in store.

Arriving in the city, I find myself amid the morning shuffle. The atmosphere is a whirl of caffeinated energy, filled with people clutching coffee cups and squinting at smartphone screens. Around me, a thousand different colognes mingle with a hint of exhaust from nearby cars.

Checking the clock, I realize I have enough time to catch the streetcar to Fisherman's Wharf, the gateway to Alcatraz. I go through the station's corridors, finally emerging into the daylight, where I can catch the F-line streetcar. A vintage, green number 162 pulls up. It's like stepping into a time machine, an old-world charm compared to the modern world around it.

As the streetcar rattles and hums along the street, I catch glimpses of the bay, its water glistening under the morning sun. My heart expands, filled with a cocktail of anticipation and a dash of worry, as if I'm standing on the edge of something monumental. Could my future life partner be standing at the dock now, waiting? Or worse, giving up and leaving?

When the streetcar finally halts at the end of the line, I scramble out, scarcely noticing the iconic crab stands and the smell of fresh seafood that usually intrigue me. Today, the only catch I'm interested in could be waiting just a ferry ride away.

Navigating through Fisherman's Wharf, I dodge selfie-taking tourists and street performers, my eyes set on Pier 33.

When I reach the ferry terminal, the clock is ticking menacingly. A glance at the large display board confirms my worry. I've missed my scheduled ferry. I suppress a groan and approach the ticket counter, where a stern-faced woman glares at me over her reading glasses.

"Listen," I ramble in my typical fashion, "I know I missed my boat, but this isn't just a sightseeing trip. It's like Tom Hanks and Meg Ryan uniting at the top of the Empire State Building in *Sleepless in Seattle*, except it's Alcatraz and, well, not a movie. I'm on a love quest here!"

The woman eyes me for a drawn-out moment, her face finally softening. "Anything for love," she says, reissuing a new ticket for a ferry that leaves in 30 minutes.

As I step back, ticket clutched in hand like a golden Willy Wonka promise of love, my stomach churns. Perhaps it's just jitters, or maybe the morning cereal has run its course, and my energy stores are empty, but I'm famished.

Either way, I snag a bag of Cheetos from a nearby vending machine and find a bench to wait.

Sitting there, I tear open the bag with more excitement than one should have for processed cheese snacks, but I can't help it. The clock is ticking, love potentially waits on an island, and darn it, Cheetos are comforting.

As I raise one toward my mouth, savoring the cheesy aroma, a seagull with impeccable aim and terrible manners swoops down from the sky. It bites my finger with a snap, snatching the Cheeto right from my hand. The sharp pain sears through me like a lightning bolt, bringing tears to my eyes.

"Ah, you winged thief!" I yell, examining my finger, expecting it to be gone with the Cheeto, but relieved it's still there. It's not a small scratch. Blood oozes steadily from the wound, and it's evident this isn't something a Band-Aid can handle.

Cursing my luck and the seagull's ancestry, I dash toward the terminal's first aid station. After evaluating the situation, a nurse suggests a quick visit to the emergency room for stitches. I gaze longingly at the ferry slowly pulling away from the dock, imagining my digital soul mate wandering around Alcatraz, perhaps wondering where his own Meg Ryan is.

THE PUNGENT SMELL of antiseptic fills my nostrils as I sit in the ER, enduring the needle and thread stitching up my adventure—and perhaps my heart. Every pull tightens the knot in my stomach, each stitch a link to the "what-ifs" I might be missing on that island.

As the nurse snips the thread and applies a bandage, I can't help but think of what my match might be doing. Is he standing alone, peering through the bars of a cold Alcatraz cell, contemplating love, and life? And here I am, bound by my own bars—a series of unfortunate events that led me to an ER room instead of into the arms of love.

Back home, I flop onto my couch, cocooned in a blanket of self-pity thicker than San Francisco fog. My finger throbs. A bag of frozen peas becomes my new best friend—great for numbing fingers but terrible at consoling broken hearts.

My eyes flicker to my phone, half-expecting it to buzz with a life-changing notification. It remains as quiet as a library on a Friday night. With a sigh, I sink further into the cushions, immersing myself in a marathon of rom-coms. I pick films where love triumphs over all adversities, where the guy rushes to the airport, stops the wedding, or climbs a mountain—just to be with the one he loves. It's ridiculous, yet I yearn for that reckless romantic gesture. Someone who'd overlook a bandaged finger and see the fun-loving spirit it's attached to.

My phone buzzes as I begin to accept that today's script doesn't include a grand love story. It's AJ.

Hey Junie, how was your day? his text reads.

My heart skips. I could tell him the truth and share my misadventures. But admitting to my crazy day feels like confessing I'd been trying to live out some cheesy romantic movie plot.

So, I reply,

Spent it in the ER. Who knew bagels could be so dangerous? I heard they're the leading cause of kitchen injuries. What about you?

Minutes later, his response arrives.

Wow, that sounds intense. My day was full of missed meetings. Hope you're okay.

Missed meetings? Is he speaking in code? I ponder the meaning but shake it off. I'm not in a position to read between the lines when I can't even navigate my own life.

I'm good. Thanks for asking. Take care.

I wonder about those "missed meetings" as my screen dims.

Several hours pass, each one stretching longer than the last. I've moved on to watching cooking shows, trying to distract myself from "what could have been" and "what if." I'm engrossed in a chef fervently slicing onions—wearing no protective gloves, I might add—when my doorbell rings.

Who could it be? No one would drop by unannounced except for Liv, and she's still not feeling great.

I open the door to find an Amazon box on my doorstep. Confused, I bring it inside and rip off the packaging tape with the finesse of a child on Christmas morning. Inside, I find a bagel cutter and a pair of mesh protective gloves.

I laugh out loud, the sound filling my empty apartment. Only AJ could turn my made-up bagel debacle into a laugh-out-loud moment.

Holding the gloves and bagel cutter as I stand there, it strikes me—maybe love isn't just about grand gestures or perfect timing. Perhaps it's also about mesh gloves and missed meetings, turning ordinary moments into extraordinary memories.

I pick up my phone and text him.

Thank you for the thoughtful gifts. You've officially made bagels a safer choice for me. I may even survive the next one.

His reply comes instantly.

Safety first, Junie. Always.

As I set the mesh gloves and bagel cutter aside, I glance at my phone, buzzing with a notification.

Challenge alert from Love Bug app!

Curious, I unlock my phone and tap the notification.

Today's challenge: List three things you want in a forever relationship.

The challenge seems simple enough, yet the words "forever relationship" make my heart race in an exciting and terrifying way.

Retreating to my comfy futon, I grab a notepad and pen, jotting down what first comes to mind. Companionship. Laughter. A sense of adventure. But the more I look at my hastily scribbled list, the more they feel like empty words, placeholders until I can fill in what forever truly means.

Suddenly, AJ's face flashes before my eyes, and warmth floods me. Could he be the one to give these words meaning? To make "forever" less of a concept and more of a reality? I dismiss the thought immediately. AJ isn't my forever. He's simply my fake for-now.

I open the app and write my deepest desires.

1. **Laughter as our love language: I want someone who appreciates my quirky humor and adds their own, creating a cacophony of giggles that resonates throughout our life together.**

2. **Endless adventure: Not just globetrotting or zip-lining over canyons, but the everyday exploits too—like cooking an extravagant dinner on a Tuesday just because, or**

spontaneously dancing in our living room.

3. **An emotional locksmith: Someone who possesses the keys to the many chambers of my heart, understanding when to give me space and when to pull me in for a life-affirming hug. A partner who doesn't just hear but listens. Not merely looks but sees.**

I input my list into the app, fingers tapping away with hope and trepidation. As I submit my answer, the app buzzes to life, revealing a new piece of information from my match. I stare at the screen, my heart thumping with anticipation. What will it be this time? A shared dream? A mutual fear? I can't wait to find out.

New insight from your match!

My thumb hesitates for a moment before I tap the screen.

1. **I want a partner who understands that life is a mixtape—a collection of highs and lows, all adding to a single, irreplaceable experience. Someone who not only celebrates the "top-chart hits" with me but**

also finds meaning in the "B-sides" that only we know.

2. **I crave a companion who treasures the quiet moments just as much as the milestones. A person who finds poetry in our morning coffee ritual, the soft whispers beneath the chaos of the city, and the shared glances that speak volumes.**

3. **And lastly, I yearn for a partner with laughter in their bones, someone who can turn our kitchen into a dance floor and our couch into the front row of a comedy show.**

I read the words repeatedly, feeling each one settle into me. Whoever this person is, they've touched on something deep, something I hadn't even realized I was yearning for but now seems essential. It's as though they've been reading my innermost thoughts, or more like they've tuned into the same hidden frequency my soul broadcasts on. And it's uncanny.

Setting aside my phone, I pull my comforter tightly around me as if I can cover myself in this newfound sense of hope. Tomorrow, I muse, letting the thought float in my mind, might be the day I meet the other half of my duet.

CHAPTER TWENTY

AJ

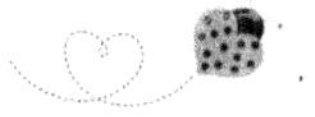

I can't believe I let him talk me into coming to the club. The thumping bass beats against my chest as I walk through the throng of people. The music seems to nudge my heart, urging it to feel something—anything—in this sea of perfume and aftershave. Flashing lights carve out fractured rainbows across faces, hands clutching drinks, eyes scanning the room for opportunity or perhaps just another body to keep them warm for the night.

Henry flags me over to our reserved table, a grin splitting his face as he leans back in mock adoration of the scene. "AJ, my man. It's a feast for the senses!"

His enthusiasm bounces off me like a rubber ball against a stone wall, leaving a chill in its wake. "Yeah, a regular buffet of life's finest," I say, forcing a smile as I settle into the plush seat.

Henry lifts his glass, filled with some amber liquid that promises more warmth than it can deliver. "To the buffet, then. May your plate never be empty."

I clink my glass against his, but the act feels mechanical. Women pass by, some throwing quick glances or flirty smiles in our direction. Typically, this would be my arena, a playground where the first questions are always the easiest. "What do you do?" followed by, "Where do you live?" Tonight, though, even as words form in my mouth to engage in these routine conversations, they taste like stale bread.

"What's the deal? You're at an all-you-can-eat buffet acting like you're on a juice cleanse," Henry says, his eyes narrowing in curiosity.

I inhale deeply, the aroma of alcohol swirling in the air tainted by an undercurrent of desperation that I can almost taste. For the first time, I question what I'm hungry for.

"There." Henry's voice jolts me from my introspection. "What about her?" He points to a woman, a sculpted vision with tumbling dark hair, walking our way. She possesses the kind of beauty that most would consider universally appealing. But tonight, all I can think of is how she isn't Junie.

"Fine. Let's see if she passes the test," I say, rising to my feet. My body moves, but my mind feels detached like I'm watching someone else. As I step into her line of sight, she offers a smile. One that doesn't reach her eyes.

"Hi, I'm Angela," she purrs, extending a hand adorned with red lacquered nails.

"AJ," I reply, feeling her fingers slide smoothly against mine. They're cool, contrasting with the warmth I felt when Junie's hands touched mine. When we walked through the gala, and at the wedding, our fingers intertwined naturally like they'd been made to fit together.

"What do you do, AJ?" Angela asks the predictable question hanging between us like stale perfume.

I answer, navigating the conversation's expected beats, yet my mind drifts. I'm struck by how her voice lacks the nuanced intonations that make Junie's speech so compelling—every word mixed with humor, intelligence, or sass, depending on her mood.

"Would you like to dance?" Angela asks, breaking into my thoughts.

"Sure," I agree, but as we make our way to the dance floor, I can't help but compare. Junie and I had danced body-to-body at the wedding, the heat between us palpable, before she broke into the funky chicken, her spontaneity making me laugh out loud. Angela moves to the beat, but her movements feel all wrong, like a song played in the wrong key.

Unable to help myself, a chuckle escapes my lips, its sound lost in the noise of the club's music and chatter.

"What's so funny?" Angela inquires, her eyebrows knotting in confusion.

"You wouldn't understand," I reply, extricating myself from the dance floor. "I have to go."

As I leave Angela standing there, perplexed, I wonder, what am I doing here when all I can think about is a sassy, red-haired psychologist who's totally off-limits?

As my car distances itself from the club, an urge to see Junie consumes me, as if pulled by an invisible thread. My hands grip the steering wheel as I speed through the night. There's a kind of gravity pulling me toward Tiburon, where she lives. The cool night air seeping through my car window tingles against my skin, each breeze like a whisper urging me on. But my mind races, too, laying out why I shouldn't be doing this.

As I approach her neighborhood, the warm, inviting glow of streetlights draws me in like metal to a magnet. It's late, but the lure is irresistible. My car hums softly, a mechanical purr that would be soothing under any other circumstance. Tonight, it sounds like hesitation.

Finally, I find myself parked outside her apartment, the engine idling like my indecisive thoughts. My gaze locks onto her window. It's dark, but I can easily picture her inside, her hair probably wild and untamed, just like the woman herself.

I hear her voice in my head. *I can't. Not while you're paying me.* And I know that if I step out of this car and go up there, I'd be crossing a line that neither of us is ready for. No, not just a line—a seismic fault that could irreversibly change the complicated, frustrating, yet undeniably captivating relationship we've built. My heart pounds, each beat an echo of my inner turmoil. With a sigh that tastes of longing, I put the car in reverse. As much as I want to be with her, I refuse to disrespect her. I won't be that guy.

The drive back is heavy, weighed down by the night's events. I let the car carry me home, but my thoughts remain at her doorstep. Tomorrow, I'll see her at the halfway meet-up for the app contest. That will have to be enough for now.

Finally, back in my apartment, I feel like a ship that's been through a storm, battered but still afloat. I toss my keys onto the counter and head straight to the kitchen, pulling a bottle of scotch from the cupboard. The amber liquid shines in the light as I pour myself a drink, its smoky aroma filling the air, promising a fleeting escape from today's emotional chaos.

I take a sip, letting the liquid warmth slide down my throat, a temporary balm for my internal struggles. The clock on the wall ticks away, its monotonous rhythm contrasting sharply with the cacophony inside my head. My phone sits on the table, silent but filled with possibilities.

Then, out of nowhere, it buzzes. My heart leaps. Could it be Junie? Or perhaps another challenge from the app, something to refocus my scattered thoughts?

I grab the phone, my fingers tingling with anticipation, but it's neither Junie nor the app. It's a message from my analyst, and my stomach tightens as I read it. Junie's app has a major bug. It's been pulled down. The words crash over me like waves, each heavier than the last.

Disbelief morphs into concern. This is a game-changer, a sinkhole opening up in the path we're both walking. According to my analyst, the app doesn't match anything but location. Any connection beyond that is pure coincidence.

The scotch morphs into liquid defeat, each sip eroding the armor of confidence I usually wear like a second skin. I set the glass down, suddenly sobered by the gravity of the situation. Tonight's internal struggle, the magnetic pull toward Junie's apartment, now feels almost trivial.

Tomorrow's meeting has just taken on a whole new level of meaning. I was prepared for emotional awkwardness, for the tension of unresolved feelings. Now, it seems, we'll also be dealing with a crisis that threatens to dismantle Junie's dreams—and possibly mine along with them.

My eyes drift toward the ceiling as if answers might be scrawled there in invisible ink. I take a deep breath, my nostrils filling with the sterile scent of my modern apartment—no home-cooked smells or comforting touches, just cold, clean space.

I think of calling her, but what would I say? "Hey, I heard your dreams might be crumbling. Need a shoulder?" Sounds crass, even in my own mind. I'll break the news tomorrow when I can see her reaction.

I'm restless, perched on the edge of my leather sofa, the glass of barely touched scotch on the coffee table. It looks inviting but smells overpowering, like liquid fire. And then I begin to think of the app. I know it's Junie's face hiding behind the avatar of a fire ant. I don't know what disappoints me more—that I won't be able to see it appear or the thought that everything we had was based on location. My gut clenches as if I've been punched. I can taste the metallic tang of dread on my tongue. My already-shaken world feels like it's coming apart at the seams. I envision the ripple effects, the catastrophe spreading through code and algorithms to influence real lives and real chances at happiness—including Junie's and mine.

A sinking feeling overtakes me, replacing the restless energy with a dense heaviness that settles in the pit of my stomach. My exhale is filled with a weariness that sinks into my bones. The soft glow of the phone casts eerie shadows on the walls, highlighting the emptiness that fills the room—and me.

I tap the numbers on the screen, dialing a flurry of emergency calls. Each one feels like a drop in an ocean of troubles, their voices filled with similar dread and urgency. Words like "immediate action," "damage control," and "public relations nightmare" clutter the air, but all I can think about is her—Junie—and how this technical hiccup might erode even the sliver of a chance we had because removing her from the contest tomorrow might mean losing her for good.

As I finish the last text, my fingers hover over Junie's contact. To call or not to call? Even Shakespeare couldn't unravel this one. I drop the phone back on the table, its screen going dark, as if it, too, knows this is a dilemma without an easy answer.

CHAPTER TWENTY-ONE

JUNIE

Walking into Steel Enterprises' bustling conference room, the atmosphere is electric, buzzing with the energy of brilliant minds and the potential for big money. But it's not just any day at the tech giant's headquarters. It's the halfway meet-up for the app contest. As I scan the room, AJ stands at the front, prepped to address the assembled contestants. He's in a tailored navy suit accentuating his broad shoulders, a crisp white shirt peeking out from beneath. His eyes, usually warm when they meet mine, now hide behind a mask of professionalism, obscuring his thoughts. God, he looks good. He always does, but today, he seems exceptionally stunning, like something from a dream.

My eyes wander to the leaderboard showcasing the contest's top apps. It takes me a second, and then another, to realize something is wrong. I skim past the top five, then the top ten, searching for any sign of Love Bug.

Nothing.

A tidal wave of confusion crashes into me, leaving me breathless. Did I miss something? Could it be a glitch?

A nudge to my arm snaps me back to reality. Ethan leans in, his voice dripping with insincere sympathy. "Tough break, huh?"

"Do you know what happened?" I prod, desperation edging my voice.

"I think you're out."

"What do you mean I'm out?" The words strike me like a sledgehammer. Is he talking about the app contest or something more? My stomach coils into painful knots, as if I'm balancing on the edge of a cliff, one misstep away from plummeting. What went wrong? Is it a new bug, a glitch, or did I just not measure up? A rush of heat climbs up my neck, and I fight the urge to bolt, to escape this room and its suffocating atmosphere. No, I can't run. I need answers, even if they're ones I don't want to hear.

He offers a casual shrug. "Might be a bug."

"Well, we knew there was a bug, but would that disqualify it? The app still functioned. So what if the ladybug didn't dance across the screen?"

Ethan's smirk widens. "Some bugs don't die easily because they're not designed that way."

AJ's voice captures the room's attention again. "I'd like to speak with Junie privately."

All eyes pivot toward me, but AJ's gaze freezes me in place. He weaves through the crowd, eyes never leaving mine. As he draws near, the rest of the room blurs into irrelevance.

I glance down at my attire—a stylish black dress

adorned with a delicate lace neckline that I've paired with the four-hundred-dollar flats. An outfit he picked out for me. What had felt like a romantic gesture now feels like a straitjacket. I yearn for the comfort of one of my quirky graphic tees, something to anchor me with its playful message—like "Under-caffeinated and Overthinking" or "Chill, It's Only Chaos." At least in a graphic tee, I'd feel more like myself. This fancy outfit makes me feel out of place and uneasy. Even these expensive flats don't make me feel grounded. Instead, I feel wobbly and unsure.

Still, there's no changing clothes or reality. As much as my stomach churns with nerves and unanswered questions, I can't let that hold me back. Especially not when AJ places his hand against my back and leads me toward his office.

"How's the finger?"

I lift it to show him my Band-Aid. "Doing better than my nerves right now."

He ushers me into his office, a space that feels like an extension of him—sleek, organized, and devoid of unnecessary frills. He directs me to a leather chair opposite his mahogany desk, and for a moment, the man I love and the enigma of a CEO meld into one figure.

He breaks the silence first. "I guess it's best to rip the Band-Aid off quickly." He frowns. "Junie, Love Bug has been disqualified from the competition."

As his words land, they carve out a hollow space within me, as if all my dreams and aspirations have been gutted. "Disqualified" echoes in my mind. I search AJ's face for some explanation, an update to fix this unexpected crash, but I only find a regretful frown. The unsettling reality sets in. There's no undo button for this.

"Disqualified? But why?" I stammer, my voice tinged with disbelief. "Is it because of the dancing bug problem? I knew about that, but surely that's not the problem."

"You knew it had a bug?"

"Yes, but it was trivial."

"It's bigger than that. Junie, the app seems to have a significant malfunction. It's not doing what you promised. Didn't you want to match people on a deeper level? It matches by location. If there's an app user within a mile radius, they're the perfect match."

"That's not possible. Location is the last thing it looks at."

"The user reviews are concerning," AJ explains, his eyes holding a mix of regret and professional detachment.

He then pivots his computer screen toward me and reads.

"One user wrote, 'Thanks for matching me with my neighbor Doris. She's 80, I'm 25. We both love bingo, but let's just say I'm not ready to be a boy toy in a retirement community.' And this one," he continues, "'Matched with a guy a mile away. Our only commonality is we both inhale oxygen. Great for respiration, bad for conversation.'"

AJ looks up from his screen. "The user reviews make it clear, Junie. The app fails to deliver its promise to make meaningful matches based on deeper values. It's a serious problem."

It's like someone's pricked my balloon of hope with a needle. The deflation is sudden and devastating. But then an idea lights up the dark recesses of my mind, like a firework in a starless sky.

"Can someone tamper with the app once it's uploaded?" My question floats in the air, heavier with implication than I intend.

He eyes me cautiously. "Are you suggesting sabotage?"

Guilt and suspicion wrestle within me. I'm torn between the possibility of betrayal from a fellow competitor and the risk of losing AJ's trust. Yet, I can't ignore the gnawing suspicion—Ethan's smirk, cryptic words, and bugs that aren't designed to die.

Finally, I speak, barely above a whisper, "I don't want to point fingers, but something isn't adding up. I can't shake the feeling that someone's meddling with Love Bug, so it loses."

AJ leans back in his chair, taking in my words, evaluating them, and most importantly, determining their impact on my fate and the competition.

AJ sighs, tapping his fingers lightly on the desk. "Junie, while I understand your concerns, you must realize that my team's job isn't to make your app perfect. Our role is to market a finished, flawless product. The fine print states that all submissions must be "sale ready." If it's not, it's disqualified. It wasn't ready, and you submitted it anyway."

His factual and unyielding words hit me like a gust of icy wind, each syllable amplifying my sense of smallness, shrinking me further into the chair that now feels more like a judgment seat.

"So, that's it? I'm just out?" My voice trembles like a fragile leaf about to fall from its branch.

"I'm afraid so," he replies as his eyes meet mine.

"Let me tell you something. That app was working perfectly when it matched us." His eyes grow wide, but I continue. "It asked the questions and sent the challenges as it should."

He smiles. "So, you are the fire ant."

I nod. "And you're a ladybug."

He shakes his head. "I'd say the app got that all wrong, but what if we were only matched because we were close in proximity and both on the app?"

"I can't believe that. What if it was functioning fine, and someone got jealous of its success and discovered a means to sabotage what was working? Isn't there a way to see that?"

AJ leans back in his chair, taking a moment to process what I've just told him. The air between us is thick with a cocktail of possibilities, each veering between hope and despair.

He finally speaks. "You really think someone would do that?"

"Yes," I say, gripping the edge of the desk to steady my shaking hands. "Someone with enough technical knowledge could corrupt the data or distort the app's programming."

He rubs his chin thoughtfully. "We do have safeguards, firewalls. But nothing is foolproof, I suppose."

"Can we check? Is there a way to trace back any unauthorized modifications?"

AJ's fingers dance across his keyboard, pulling up lines of code on the screen. My eyes fixate on each movement, my heart pounding with every scroll. Could this be the sliver of a chance I've been hoping for or just another pathway to disappointment?

He pauses, his eyes narrowing as they scan the dense text. "I don't see any obvious tampering, but I'm not a developer. We'd have to get our tech team to do a deep dive, and even then, finding proof would be a needle in a haystack."

"So, what does that mean for me?" My voice is barely above a whisper.

AJ locks eyes with me, a new gravity in his gaze. "Even if we find evidence of sabotage, the rules are clear. The app must be 'sale ready,' and it wasn't. I can't bend the guidelines, even if I wanted to."

All of a sudden, the room feels cavernous, and I am insignificant within it. The shiny marble tile, the sleek desk, and even the modern art on the wall become mocking symbols of a world where I apparently don't belong. My eyes wander to a corner of AJ's desk, where a promotional poster for the app contest lies. "Turn Your Dream into Reality," it reads, but it feels more like my dream has been jolted awake and tossed out a window.

"I see," I murmur, the words like ashes in my mouth. Every inch of this luxurious office suddenly feels suffocating. But as AJ remains silent, something within me snaps. Enough of feeling small, enough of shrinking away.

I rise to my feet, my dress clinging to me like a second skin, an armor of vulnerability and strength. "AJ, you can't possibly think that our connection was just a bug in the system, a coding error?" His eyes shift, meeting mine for the first time with a vulnerability he rarely shows. "What we had was real, whether you want to admit it or not," I continue, my voice unwavering. "Your distrust in love, in anything that doesn't come with a set of terms and conditions, is clouding your judgment." He opens his mouth to speak, but I cut him off. "If you can sit there and tell me that Love Bug, the very app that brought us together, is faulty because of some fine print, then maybe it's not the app that's flawed. Maybe it's your perspective."

His gaze locks onto mine, and for a fleeting second, I see something there— recognition, perhaps, or even regret. "I can't break the rules, even for you. Not even if I wanted to."

Regaining my composure, I press on, remembering the painting—"The Boy in the Red Vest," his favorite. "Remember your favorite piece of art? Well, there's something to be said about it. He may be alone, but at least he's authentic. He's not hiding behind fine print or legalese. Maybe it's time that boy learns to take risks with his heart, like he's done so successfully with his finances."

"I'm not that boy," he says.

"Open your eyes. I'm big enough to admit I am the

chaos in my favorite painting. I don't hide from it. I embrace it."

With that, I head toward the door.

"Junie, wait, my mother invited us to lunch on Friday."

I stop dead in my tracks, wondering what is going on. The man just blew up my life and still wants me to pretend?

"Are you serious? After all this, you still want to parade me around as your pretend girlfriend?" My disbelief mingles with a newfound sense of liberation.

AJ's eyes meet mine, searching for acceptance, forgiveness, and maybe even love. "She likes you, and it's important to her."

"Your mother will have to deal with disappointment, just like the rest of us," I say, my voice steely yet sorrowful. "I refuse to live a lie anymore. Especially with you."

My words hang between us, irrevocable and final. I turn once more, leaving behind not just AJ and his fancy office but also a love that could have been—but never was.

I pause before stepping out the door, drawing in a shaky breath as I look back one final time. I stop, hand on the door. "I thought I loved you, but it's hard to love someone too scared to love himself—or anyone else. One day, you might find your own Doris—someone within a mile's radius, sharing nothing more than proximity and perhaps a fondness for bingo. I hope you get more than that." He seems to flinch as if my words have struck a deep chord within him. "But it's your loss because I would've loved you wholly, fiercely, and without reservation. But I won't be your prop in a make-believe relationship when there was so much that was real to explore." I square my shoulders, walk out the door, and march toward Ethan, my eyes locked onto his. The moment he sees me, his conversation with another contestant falters. I don't give him the chance to excuse himself.

"Ethan, we need to talk. Now." My voice is a blade, cutting through the air.

He looks at me, his eyes narrowing, but he can't ignore the urgency in my voice. "Alright, Junie. What's so important?"

I yank him aside, distancing us from the crowd to ensure our words don't carry. "I know what you did to Love Bug. You sabotaged the algorithm, didn't you?"

His face goes white for a split second before he regains his composure. "What are you talking about? Why would I sabotage your app?"

"Because you couldn't stand the idea of sharing success. You'd rather have all of a losing app than a third of one that's actually going places. Remember what you said? 'You know, some bugs don't die easily because they're not designed that way.'"

"I was talking about real bugs, like cockroaches." His eyes shift away from mine, but not quickly enough. "I don't want any part of Love Bug."

I lock eyes with him, my resolve unwavering. "If you truly want nothing to do with Love Bug, then put it in writing. Right here, right now."

He looks at me. "You're serious?"

"As serious as a fire ant," I reply, pulling out a crumpled bus ticket and a pen from my bag. "Write that despite contributing to the code, you relinquish all financial rights to Love Bug. Sign it."

He hesitates, the pen hovering over the paper. Finally, with a resigned sigh, he writes the words down and signs his name with a flourish.

I snatch the ticket back. "You've officially severed your ties with Love Bug, and with that, any chance of sharing in its future success."

"A third of nothing is still nothing," he says.

As I walk away. I can't help but feel the emptiness grow within me. But there's also a sense of liberation, of cutting ties with Ethan and more so with AJ that were never truly fastened. I may have lost this contest, but I refuse to lose myself.

CHAPTER TWENTY-TWO

AJ

I sit there, still as a statue, staring at the now-closed door. The air in the office thickens as if charged with electricity, and my knuckles whiten as I grip the edge of the desk. Did Junie just say she loved me? My chest constricts, as if the walls of the room are closing in on me.

I swivel my chair around to face the window, but the expansive city view does little to distract me. Instead, my thoughts drift back to what just happened. As she said those words, the look in her eyes wasn't just that of a wounded competitor. It was the look of someone who had lost something much more significant. And what's worse, I think I've lost it, too.

"Love," I mutter to myself. The word hangs in the air, unfamiliar and unsettling. I've dealt with mergers and acquisitions, business strategies, and investments, but this? This is beyond me.

I rake my fingers through my hair, the tension building up like a pressure cooker. Lost and adrift, I grapple with the irony that a man who prides himself on having all the answers now has none. It dawns on me that I may have disqualified the one thing that was rare and genuine.

She's pierced the one set of armor I never knew I wore—a fear of intimacy masked as bravery everywhere else. And now, I'm starting to wonder what the greater risk is—letting someone in or shutting out love altogether.

The light tap on my office door stirs the silence. For a split second, I hope it's Junie, and she's come back to sort things out. Leaping up from my chair, I rush to the door and yank it open, only to find Sarah, my head analyst, standing there instead.

"Can we talk?" she asks, scrutinizing my face as if attempting to decode the chaos of emotions I'm struggling to hide.

"Yeah, sure," I mutter, stepping aside to let her enter. "Have a seat."

Sarah sits down across from my desk, her posture stiff, all business. "Love Bug's disqualification may not bother you, but it's weighing on me. You were against it from the start, but when it's working, it's pure genius."

"I wasn't against it." The lie tastes bitter on my tongue. "Fine, I didn't think it had a chance."

"Don't you know ... love always wins." Sarah shakes her head, her face grave. "Anyway, I took the liberty of diving into Love Bug's code when everything went to hell. There's something you should know. There was an update right after the app launched. It was buried under a hundred layers of code, but we found it, and we peeled back the layers to Ethan's IP address."

My heart skips a beat. Junie was right. Her app was sabotaged. But how can I reinstate her without tarnishing the company's reputation? The decision hangs over me like a suspended anvil, ready to drop.

"The implications of this are heavy," Sarah continues, eyeing me carefully. "If word gets out that the contest was compromised, it could spell trouble for Steel Enterprises. We'd lose credibility. But if we don't address it, we're condoning sabotage. It's a lose-lose situation."

I lean back in my chair, my mind racing. "And if I reinstate Love Bug, what then? How does that look for us? For her?"

"You'd be correcting a wrong, but it might appear as though you're showing favoritism, given your ... relationship with Junie."

"Does everyone know?" The words slip out before I can filter them. I was sure we'd maintained a façade of professionalism, leaving our personal lives—real or imagined—out of the office space.

Sarah hesitates, then shrugs. "Let's just say that people can sense things, even if they can't put their finger on exactly what's happening."

I mull over her words, grappling with the truth they carry. What started as a charade between Junie and me had morphed into something I couldn't quite name yet couldn't ignore. The way my pulse quickens when her name lights up my phone, the warmth that flows through me when our eyes meet, the unspoken conversations we have in mere glances—it all points to something real, something meaningful. Was this how love felt? A steady glow that gradually intensified, rather than a sudden blaze that consumed everything in its path.

But now that glow felt dimmed, shadowed by doubt, and marred by choices I wish I could undo. I hadn't supported her in the way she deserved, and my failure had cast a cloud over us.

Sarah's eyes narrow just slightly. "People might question the integrity of the contest. It would also raise questions about our security measures, that someone could tamper with the code in the first place."

As she lays out the tangled web of complexities, I can't help but think about the look on Junie's face as she left my office—her eyes, once warm, now cold with disillusionment. She had looked at me as if I were a stranger. Perhaps I had become one to her.

As I murmur Junie's words—"It's hard to love someone too scared to love himself—or anyone else"—it hits me like a freight train. She's right on two counts. I failed to support her work, ambition, and app—one form of not loving her back. And emotionally? I've been holding back, too. That's the second betrayal. In failing her professionally, I've also failed her personally. And in that moment, I understand just how much I've lost.

"What will you do?" Sarah asks, breaking into my thoughts.

The options lay before me, none without consequence. But isn't that what life—and love—is all about? Taking risks and facing the consequences?

"I need to think," I say finally, looking up to meet Sarah's gaze. "But whatever I decide, it'll be in the service of setting things right—on all fronts."

Sarah nods, rising from her seat. "I'll leave you to it, then."

As she exits the room, closing the door softly behind her, I'm left alone with my thoughts and a decision that could redefine not just my professional life but my personal one, too. What would that lone boy from my painting do? Would he dare to risk his heart?

For the first time, I find myself hoping he would. Because if he could take that leap, then maybe, just maybe, so could I.

IN THE CONFERENCE ROOM, flanked by my top advisors, I open up the meeting with a new concept called "Operation Fire Ant." The name is fitting. Fire ants are resilient and industrious, and their impact far exceeds their size—just like Junie.

While the app challenge is publicly touted as a launchpad for emerging talents, it's an open secret that the real winner is always the corporation. We gain more than we give, benefiting from fresh insights and revolutionary ideas. This year, though, it's not just about business. It's personal. Junie has something that can't be quantified yet is immeasurably valuable. It's become painfully clear. She doesn't need me as much as I need her. Whether her app works or not is irrelevant to me because she and I work, or at least we did until I booted her from the competition.

They say it takes a village. As we begin Operation Fire Ant, I feel that more than ever. This isn't just about business. It's a collective effort to do more than just resolve a bug or a competition hiccup. I'm working to bring Junie back—not into the competition, but into my open arms.

As I sit there, a decision looming ahead of me, I understand that courage doesn't just involve taking a chance on a business venture or a new idea. Real courage isn't just wagering on the success of a project. It's the pulse-quickening, gut-churning risk of placing your heart in someone else's hands. It's letting your walls come down and hoping—against all logic and experience—that things will be different this time.

JUNIE

I unlock my apartment door, kicking off my shoes as soon as I cross the threshold. Today has been a rollercoaster of emotional highs and lows, and I need to talk to Liv. We've been texting since I boarded the bus home, but this conversation deserves more than mere bits of text on a screen.

Just as I settle onto the couch, there's a knock at the door. I open it to find Liv holding a triple-decker hamburger from my favorite guilty-pleasure joint and a dozen cookies from Pies Before Guys. "For you," she says, pushing them into my hands.

"Wow, a hamburger? You really are worried about me," I say, setting the food on the coffee table.

"As soon as you said hello, I knew it was a hamburger kind of day," she replies. "And while I'm opposed to eating meat, I'm also opposed to my best friend feeling like crap. So today, the cows are taking one for Team Junie."

I laugh, appreciating the irony as I see Liv take out her own vegan cookies from her bag. "Well, at least we can share the moment, if not the cookies."

"You got it," she grins, tearing open the package. "Somehow, these vegan cookies taste much better with you here."

We share a laugh and eagerly bite into our respective cookies, indulging in that simple act. If today has taught me anything, it's that life has a whimsical, unpredictable rhythm that can shift your world on its axis when you least expect it. In moments like these, dessert shouldn't just be an afterthought. It deserves to be a first act, a small rebellion against life's uncertainties.

I let the flavors dance on my tongue, taking a moment to savor the delicate blend of sugar, butter, and love crafted into each bite. And as the sweetness seeps into my senses, a warm realization blooms within me. Some things in life are genuine in their simplicity. Like this cookie, baked without artificial enhancers or complex ingredients, my friendship with Liv requires no additives or embellishments to be authentic. In its most fundamental form, it is a thing of pure, straightforward beauty—a comfort that asks for nothing in return yet gives so much.

"Now spill," Liv says, setting her cookie down. "I need every detail."

As I recount the day's events—the meeting with AJ, the look in his eyes, the disqualification of Love Bug, the words left unsaid, and the feelings that went unsorted—I can see Liv's face fluctuating between empathy and fury.

When I finish, she leans back, digesting more than just her cookie.

"You want me to toilet-paper his office? Or maybe sign him up for endless junk mail? The possibilities are endless," she says.

"As tempting as those sound, I'll pass. Hurting someone just because they hurt you never solves anything."

Liv nods, her eyes meeting mine in a moment of deep understanding. "You're wiser than you give yourself credit for, Junie."

"In moments like this, maybe," I admit, "but wisdom has a funny way of playing hide-and-seek when you need it most."

With that, Liv raises her vegan cookie in a toast. "To finding wisdom, even in its most elusive corners."

"And to friendship, the best guide through any maze," I add, clinking my full-butter cookie against her vegan one. In that instant, I know that no matter what lies ahead, I won't have to face it alone.

"I'll spare the toilet paper," she concedes. "But the offer's always on the table. A girl's got to have options, you know?"

"Enough about me, how are you feeling?" I ask, taking a bite of my burger.

Liv takes a deep breath. "I got the all-clear from the doctor. No more mono. I can reenter life as I knew it." She puckers her lips. "These bad boys are ready for some action."

"You've been missed," I say, relief washing over me. "Definitely by me, and probably more by the pizza guy."

Liv sighs dramatically, a wistful expression taking over her face. "Ah, the pizza guy. He had all the right toppings but look where that got me." She raises an eyebrow, the corners of her mouth twitching into a playful smile. "So, what will you do now?" she asks.

"I'll go back to looking for a job," I say, taking another bite of the burger. "You brought me a burger, Liv. That's true love. Too bad AJ's love has limits."

Liv shrugs. "Well, thanks to him, at least you have some great interview clothes."

I gasp, reminded of the obligation I'd forgotten. I gobble up the last bite. "I need to return those clothes."

Grabbing Liv by the hand, I rush to my room and yank open the closet door. Inside is a curated collection of dresses, skirts, and blouses—gifts from AJ, each with a hypothetical future.

I pick up a silk cocktail dress the color of a tropical sea, and my eyes meet Liv's. "This is what I would have worn to a gallery opening, where AJ would introduce me as the woman who stole his heart," I say, the words thick in my throat.

"And this," I continue, lifting a tailored suit set, "was for the corporate parties where I wouldn't understand anyone's job titles but would smile just the same."

Liv watches me, her eyes full of unspoken emotion. "Junie, you don't have to—"

"But I do, Liv," I interrupt. "I can't owe him anything, not even a vision of a future that won't exist."

Taking a deep breath, I place the items into a bag, the dreams they represented neatly folded away.

"We have to return these," I say, my voice tinged with finality. "Liv, will you come with me? I can't do this alone."

"Of course," she replies, her eyes meeting mine with understanding. "We'll return every stitch."

Thirty minutes later, we navigate the polished aisles of Saks. I request the return, and Avis, the sales associate who helped me before, helps me now. She raises her eyebrows but remains professional when I ask her to give me a total for the things I've worn already and can't return. She goes to the computer and pulls up the order.

"I remember how he looked at you when you tried on that dress. Like a cat who had just found the cream," Avis says.

"Turns out, too much dairy can upset the stomach."

Avis sighs. When she tallies the cost for the worn items, my heart plummets.

I stare at the number, each digit hammering into my sense of reality.

Avis tilts her head sympathetically. "I thought things would work out for you. You two seemed perfect."

I shake my head. "Well, fairy tales rarely come true. I'm not Julia Roberts, he's no Richard Gere, and this story definitely isn't Pretty Woman." I look at the receipt again, feeling the enormity of the number there. "Now, if you'll excuse me, I have some debts to settle."

I find Liv next to a Chanel display.

"Is everything alright?" she whispers.

"It was more than I imagined," I mutter, looking at the receipt. "Way more."

Outside, I take a deep breath, my thoughts racing. How can I pay AJ back? My eyes drift across the street to the pawn shop, and my thoughts go to my grandmother's ring.

"Junie, you're not thinking—"

"I have to, Liv," I say, interrupting her. "I have to go home and get the ring."

When we return to my apartment, I head straight to my jewelry box. My hands shake as I pick up Grandma's wedding set. As I lift the rings from their velvet perch, they feel heavy in my palm—like they're loaded with the gravity of my decision. This was my fallback, my just-in-case, a token of unconditional love that I'd always thought would grace my hand on my wedding day. Yet here I am, about to exchange this irreplaceable piece of my heritage for a chance to settle the balance with AJ. And as my fingers close around the cool metal, I wonder if some debts are too large to repay.

"You sure about this?" Liv asks, her voice tinged with concern.

"I need to be free of him." I look into her eyes. "Even if it costs me everything."

THE PAWN SHOP has a musty smell, a mixture of old books, rusting metal, and broken dreams. I open the box to show the shop owner my grandmother's wedding ring set.

"I always thought I'd wear these on my wedding day," I tell Liv as the owner examines the rings under a magnifying glass. Her eyes meet mine, and in that moment, we share a collective grief for dreams that have died.

Liv reaches over and squeezes my hand. "This is a big sacrifice, Junie."

"I'd rather keep my dignity than a beautiful dream that's out of reach. You know me, Liv. I can't bear owing him anything."

The shop owner offers a price that makes my stomach drop. It's far less than the rings are worth, far less than they mean to me, but it's enough to settle my debt with AJ.

I nod, authorizing him to go ahead. He places the rings in a drawer, out of sight but not out of mind.

"Here you go," he says, counting the bills into my trembling hand.

I fold the money carefully and hand it to Liv. "Can you give this to AJ? Facing him again is beyond me."

Liv's eyes lock with mine, shadowed by the moment's significance. "For you, anything," she says, accepting the bills. It's one thing to share secrets and comfort food, it's another to become an emotional courier, delivering the final payment on a love that can never be.

"Mind if I deliver it in a few days? I have appointments and I need to show my face to my parents. They probably think I've been abducted by aliens or run off to join a cult."

I chuckle at her exaggerated excuses. She's just looking out for me or perhaps hoping I'll reclaim the money I so clearly need. "The sooner, the better, but take your time."

"I'll make sure he gets it," Liv promises, tucking the money safely into her bag.

"Thank you," I choke out, my voice catching.

She hugs me, and for a moment, I allow myself to be enveloped in her warmth—in the love of a friend who'd do anything for me.

As Liv and I part ways on the bustling sidewalk outside the pawn shop, I feel a deep sense of closure and yet an equally deep emptiness. I turn back toward home, walking through a cityscape that looks the same but feels irreversibly changed.

CHAPTER TWENTY-FOUR

AJ

I'm seated behind my desk, phone clenched in my hand, typing, erasing, typing again. Every apology feels hollow, every explanation like an excuse. How do you apologize for breaking someone's trust, perhaps even their heart?

My thumbs hover over the glowing screen. The cursor blinks in and out as if challenging me to type anything that could start mending the rift between Junie and me. I've tried calling her for three days, and she won't answer. I even went to her apartment and knocked on her door, but she didn't open it. Now, confined to text, words escape me. Each deleted message is proof of my growing desperation.

First attempt:

Junie, I'm so sorry. Can we talk?

No, too simple. Erase.

Second attempt:

I messed up. I never meant to hurt you. Please, let's talk.

Too desperate. Erase.

Third attempt:

I realize now that my actions cost me more than I could ever have imagined. I lost something invaluable—your trust.

Too formal. Sounds like a corporate apology letter. Erase.

I set my phone down, frustrated. Each message feels like throwing a bucket of water on a forest fire—pointless and inadequate.

My intercom buzzes, breaking my spiraling thoughts.

"Mr. Steel, there's a woman here to see you. Someone named Liv Kato."

I raise an eyebrow. Liv? The only Liv I know of is Junie's vegan friend, but why would she come to see me?

"Send her in," I say, curiosity getting the best of me.

The door swings open, and a woman with vibrant eyes and a confident stride walks in. There's something about her demeanor that says she means business.

"Mr. Steel, I'm Liv," she says.

I stand. "Nice to meet you, Liv. What can I do for you?"

Liv takes a seat opposite me, her eyes unyielding. She reaches into her bag and produces a wad of bills, methodically unfolding each one as she sets them on the gleaming surface of my desk. The money lies there, crisp, and flat.

For a moment, I think she's trying to bribe me—to reinstate Junie's app into the competition. If only it could be that easy.

"Your money won't make a difference," I say, my voice colored with disbelief.

"It's not my money. It's yours," she says, pushing the pile of bills closer to me.

Confusion muddles my mind. "What do you mean?"

"Junie doesn't want to owe you anything," she says, and it's as if her words materialize into a fist that punches straight into my chest. The air leaves my lungs in a rush. My heart threatens to stop beating. "You should have seen a credit on your card for the clothes she could return. This covers the rest."

I focus on the stack of bills sitting on my desk. "I don't understand. Everything I bought for Junie is hers. She doesn't owe me anything." My voice trails off into a whisper, as though speaking louder might make this real.

Liv's eyes meet mine, unbending yet filled with secondhand sorrow. "Junie's cutting ties and wants to settle any debts she has with you." Her words land like a gut punch, pushing me into the depths of my chair. "So, what now? Does she hate me? Is that it?" I sputter, half-expecting, half-dreading her response.

Liv's lips curl into a wistful half-smile, touched with a sadness that isn't her own. "Junie doesn't have the capacity for hate, not even now. You're lucky there—she even stopped me from TP'ing your high-rise temple."

As Liv speaks, I'm gripped by an overwhelming need for Junie to be the one saying these words. Liv's voice feels like a placeholder, a beta version of an app missing its key features.

In this instant, a gnawing inadequacy grabs me, emphasizing how ill-equipped I am to be what Junie needs.

My accomplishments—the money, the high-rise office—appear absurdly insignificant. Liv's commentary amplifies what's lacking—Junie's voice, her emotional depth, the unspoken things only she can bring to our world. The emptiness echoes louder than any success, making me question the worth of everything I've built.

"How did she come up with the money?" I ask, my voice laced with a new urgency but dreading the answer.

Liv hesitates. "I shouldn't tell you this, but you should know how far she will go to make things right. Junie pawned her grandmother's wedding ring set."

My heart drops to the floor. The room seems to contract, the walls inching closer as if to suffocate me. "She did what?" I can barely articulate the words, my throat tightening.

"Yeah. That ring was supposed to be her 'happily ever after.' And now it's gone, just like her dreams of making it in this city, her dreams with you," Liv adds, her voice breaking, but not as much as my heart does now.

"I need to fix this."

"Yes, you do, but why do you care?" Liv fires back, her voice laced with bitterness.

It is a question so simple yet so complex. I run my fingers through my hair, a mix of frustration and desperation overtaking me. "Because I love her, Liv. I love Junie, and I've royally messed this up."

Liv's eyes widen, studying my face as if searching for any sign of deceit. "Love's a big word, especially for you."

"How would you know?"

"Because Junie and I talk. She's shared your, let's say, skeptical views on love. Not exactly a fairy-tale believer, are you?"

"That was before Junie. She's more important to me than any business deal, competition—more than anything." My voice grows urgent, tinged with desperation, pleading for a lifeline, for some way to mend the fracture between us. "Tell me how to fix this."

Liv snorts, her eyes meeting mine. "Fix it? If you're serious, you're looking at Olympic-level groveling, my friend. We're talking Simone Biles-level gymnastic contortions of remorse."

Her words bring a short, dry chuckle from me, the mood lightening just a sliver. "I am serious, and I'll do what it takes. I'm ready to leap, flip, and stick the landing."

"You'd better because if you truly love Junie, you will have to show her, not just tell her. She needs grand gestures, epic moments," Liv says, her face turning earnest. "But you should also articulate that sentiment to her because she doesn't have a clue."

"I will, but what about these grand gestures?" I lean in. "What would show her I mean it?"

Liv hesitates as if weighing whether to share a secret recipe. "Junie thrives on symbols. Big, undeniable symbols that she can hold on to. Words fade. Actions don't."

I nod, contemplating the gravity of what she's saying. "I think I know just the thing." My lips curl into a determined smile.

"Good luck, AJ. You'll need it," Liv warns as she rises, heading for the door.

"I know," I say, the implication of the task settling in, matching the heaviness in my chest. But as the door closes behind her, I'm already busy formulating my plan to either restore everything I've lost or ruin myself completely. And for the first time in a long time, I'm hoping for the former with a desperation that startles even me.

Liv's hand pauses on the doorknob, her expression turning thoughtful again. "Listen, if you're really all-in on Junie, the things that matter to her must matter to you. You're from different worlds. She worries that the gap between your bank accounts will always be a gap between you two."

I feel a pang of guilt. That's my doing. I gave her that notion. "I see what you mean," I say softly.

Liv turns back to me, "If you want to stand any chance, you need to bridge that gap. But it can't be you swooping in like some corporate prince. She needs skin in the game. That app was her chance to shine. And honestly, it was genius. If you think you got matched by location, you're an idiot. She didn't want any match. She wanted Mr. Right. That girl pared down her desires to a T so there would be no mistaking anything. If you showed up, it was because you were made for her, and you have to believe that in your heart." She exits and closes the door.

I immediately press the intercom button to call Mary.

"Operation Fire Ant needs an update. Get Sarah and the team together. She and Caesar are going to Junie's. This has to be about Junie and for her. But make it fast."

"Are you sure about this, boss?" Mary's voice crackles through the speaker. "Won't this set a bad precedent?"

My original plan was to get a venture capitalist to look into her app and see if he was interested, but that could take months, and Junie doesn't have months, and neither do I. I want Junie back now.

"We've already allocated server time and resources to her for two weeks. Once it's up and running perfectly, pull out. She'll operate it alone," I reply, cutting the call short. "Just tell her that Steel Enterprises believes she has potential."

With the plan in motion, a sense of urgency replaces the heaviness clouding me. We'll make the app perfect, but then it's all on her. The server time and the resources are still hers to use. Whatever revenue she generates from this point will be her own victory, earnings, and path to financial independence.

Maybe this could be the grand gesture Liv was talking about, the symbol that shows I'm taking what matters to Junie seriously. By leveling the playing field, I'm not just whispering but shouting my belief in her dreams, her worth, her untapped potential.

And perhaps, if I'm lucky, she'll see it as a sign that

our worlds aren't too far apart to merge, that love doesn't measure bank accounts, and that we could build something priceless together. The selfish part of me wants that app back up today to see if it still matches us. The logical side of me says it won't, but the dreamer in me says, as ridiculous as it might seem, Junie Parker is the one.

CHAPTER TWENTY-FIVE

JUNIE

My eyes blur, my phone screen turning into an unfocused haze. Days have passed, and each one brings with it more—more longing for AJ. He's messaged me dozens of times, but I can't bring myself to answer. I'm afraid I'd give in too quickly. I have to remind myself that I hate him. But even thinking that tastes like a bitter lie. I could never hate him when I love him so much. There was so much potential with him. Without him, there's nothing. Even my grandmother's ring is gone in my futile attempt to erase him from my memory. A keepsake I once imagined wearing on my wedding day is now a lost relic, pawned off in a desperate attempt to banish him from my life, erase how his lips felt against mine or how his arms held me when we danced. I remove a tissue from the box on my nightstand, dab at my tears, and consider a text to Liv. I have so many questions and so few answers. But before I can unlock my phone, a knock at the door interrupts my spiral of thoughts.

Anticipating Liv's face—as if she received my unspoken plea for company—I shove my phone into my pocket and dash to the door. When it swings open, I find not Liv but Sarah and Caesar from AJ's team standing on my threshold. Taut smiles grace their lips, their eyes a complicated mix of determination and awkwardness.

"Can we come in?" Sarah asks, her gaze flicking past me to the disarray inside my apartment. "We have something to discuss."

"Uh, sure," I reply, stepping back to let them in. "What brings you here?"

My heart pounds with a curious blend of dread and expectancy. Despite his apologies, did AJ dispatch them for some final, soul-crushing errand? As they follow me into the apartment, I push aside empty coffee cups and a tangle of charging cables from the table, clearing space for whatever comes next.

"We came to help," Sarah says, settling into a chair. She takes a laptop from her bag and puts it on the table. "You still have server time allocated. We can get your app back on its feet."

The room brightens momentarily as if the universe is adjusting the contrast on my miserable day. "So, am I back in the competition?" I ask, leaning forward.

Caesar shakes his head, his expression a grim cocktail of apology and finality. "No," he replies, and my hopes plummet like a falling star.

"But," Sarah interjects, "once we fix the bug, any money the app makes is yours."

A maelstrom of emotions tugs at my heart. "Does it

even matter?" I murmur, almost to myself. "I've already lost so much. My hopes, dreams, and everything around me, including my grandmother's wedding ring set, are gone. I had to pawn it."

Sarah's eyes narrow. "You pawned your grandma's ring? Where did you do it? Why?"

"At a pawn shop close to Saks. I had some debts that couldn't wait."

"I think we can help." Sarah's eyes soften as she drapes her arm around my shoulders. "We think you've got potential, kid. And so does AJ. He's the reason we're here." It's as if she's channeling the movie.

Hearing Sarah echo the famous line, my emotions undergo a seismic shift. I've been swept into a movie scene where everything pivots on a single phrase. Could I, too, have my own Richard Gere moment, where everything shifts toward a happier ending?

My thoughts wander to AJ. Unlike Richard Gere's iconic role, AJ hadn't scaled ladders or brandished umbrellas like a white knight coming to my rescue. No, he sent Sarah and Caesar. Was it just a business move? Or maybe he felt more but didn't know how to show it? His eyes told me he wanted me, but did that want include the rest of me—my hopes, my dreams, my messes?

And then a new thought sneaks in. What if guilt fuels his actions? Maybe he sent them to ease his conscience, not because he believes in me but because his actions need absolution. Does it even matter? Love and belief are great, but my wallet's on a diet right now, and it's not the good kind. Is this what they call a Hail

Mary in the last seconds of a game when you're crossing your fingers and praying the quarterback has good aim?

The room's energy transforms, heavy with a sense of unanticipated grace, second chances, and hidden allies. My heart, weighed down by doubt for so long, flutters with cautious optimism.

Huh—is the universe actually throwing me a bone here? For the first time in forever, I'm not just waiting for the other shoe to drop. Maybe, just maybe, my life's not a total dumpster fire after all.

"Are you game?" Caesar asks.

The words hang in the air. I feel light-headed but manage a nod.

"Alright, let's do this."

"Let's get you making money so you can buy that ring back," Sarah suggests, plugging in her laptop.

The idea of reclaiming my grandmother's ring stirs something inside me like a dormant seed, suddenly deciding it's time to grow. Yet there's also a knot of disbelief—could it be that simple?

"Let's get this party started," I manage to say despite the emotional whirlwind.

We huddle around my tiny dining table, its wood surface cluttered with remnants of a life put on hold—unused notebooks, scattered pens, and coffee-stained papers. Sarah flips open her laptop, and Caesar starts mumbling tech jargon as he sifts through lines of code on his tablet. The atmosphere is thick with concentration.

After what feels like an eternity but is probably just

minutes, Caesar lets out a low whistle. "Well, I'll be damned. It's not one bug but two."

"By Ethan, I presume?" Sarah narrows her eyes at the screen.

"Who else?" Caesar says, scrolling through more text. "I've removed the bugs. It should be clean now. Let's test it out." They start a series of tests as I watch lines of text scroll up the screen.

A flush of indignation rises within me, hotter than any fever. To think that Ethan would stoop so low. It's like discovering a worm in an apple you've been savoring. "What happened to him?"

Sarah closes her laptop with a satisfying snap and grins. "His app got disqualified, and he owes us for all the man hours we spent perfecting his launch. Karma is digital these days, it seems."

The news lands with a peculiar sense of satisfaction, like seeing a villain fall into his own trap in a movie. Yet, my heart remains restless, grappling with many unfinished feelings and what-ifs. It's a strange blend of vindication and loss, as if I've won a battle but I'm still losing the war. "You know, I was dragged into this mess, kicking, and screaming, all thanks to Liv. At first, I was all, 'Me, represent our app? Yeah, right.' But here I am. And yeah, things went south and got all tangled and crazy, but I've also surprised myself. I stood up in front of people and pitched something I believe in. I squared off with AJ, Mr. Tech Tycoon himself. And as much as I wanted to crawl into a hole some days, I didn't. I learned to back myself up and take myself seriously, even when it felt like the world was pointing and laughing. Despite the chaos, I kinda found pieces of myself I didn't know were there."

"You should be proud of yourself. The point is—you're still in the game. We can't get you back into the competition, but we've set things right. Anything the app makes from now on is yours. You're a free agent in the tech world."

"But being a free agent doesn't help me buy back my grandmother's ring," I murmur, my eyes drifting to my ring finger. The loss feels like an unhealed wound, a constant reminder of dreams deferred and hopes dashed.

Sarah covers my hand with her own. "Let's ensure you earn enough and more to get that ring back."

The thought fills me with newfound determination, like a phoenix rising from the ashes of its own despair.

As Sarah and Caesar collect their things, I walk them to the door, my heart teetering between newfound hope and lingering doubts. "Thank you for everything," I say, my words full of genuine warmth.

Sarah gives me a parting hug, her grip promising unspoken solidarity. "Remember, Junie, this isn't over. Your app has a future, and so do you."

Caesar offers a farewell nod, his face mirroring the quiet strength of his convictions. "Don't forget, you've got this. You've got yourself."

As they step out, another figure appears at the entrance. It's Liv, showing up when I think the day's rollercoaster of emotions has hit its final loop. "Liv! Perfect timing," I say, pulling her into a hug as Sarah and Caesar exchange nods and disappear down the hall.

"Come in, come in. Oh my gosh, you will not believe what just happened."

As Liv and I sink into the comfort of the living room, the day's emotional residue still clings to us, like fog yet to be burned off by the morning sun. I recount the day's surprises, the rollercoaster that ended neither in a crash nor jubilant victory but somewhere in the middle—a plateau of possibilities.

"So, spill the beans. How did your meeting with AJ go?" I probe, my curiosity bubbling over.

Liv's eyes lock onto mine as she leans forward, her voice tinged with a knowing warmth. "Junie, AJ loves you."

I burst into laughter, the sound a strange mix of skepticism and yearning. "Love? Oh, come on! Fixing a buggy app and sending Sarah and Caesar isn't love. It's business diplomacy."

"Junie, listen to me," Liv says, locking eyes with me. "I talked to AJ. I understand he's not speaking your love language right now, but trust me, he's catching on."

"I don't know, Liv. Words are cheap. What if this is temporary, and he returns to being Mr. Tech Tycoon, who doesn't have time for anyone else?"

Liv tightens her grip on my hand. "I laid it out for him. Told him if he doesn't step up his game, he will lose you for good. And you know what? I could see it in his eyes. He's planning something. He didn't spill the beans, but believe me, he got the message."

"Am I supposed to sit around, waiting for signs and signals?"

"No," Liv says. "You live your life, and you be you. But keep an eye out. I feel you'll be seeing some grand gestures from his end soon. If you're open to it, that is."

As I hold Liv's gaze, a sense of resolution settles over me. Whatever comes next, I'll face it. "Okay," I say finally, a smile tugging at the corners of my lips. "Let's see where life takes me."

CHAPTER TWENTY-SIX

AJ

I'm hunched over my desk, scrolling through a monotonous spreadsheet that might as well be ancient hieroglyphics. The numbers are blending together, but I keep my eyes trained on the screen, reluctant to tear myself away. That's until Sarah barges into my office, flinging the door open with enough force to open a new doorway on the wall it hits.

"AJ, the app is back up and running," she declares, her eyes alight with enough energy to power the Bay Area for a week.

I lean back in my chair, my shoulders untensing for the first time in hours. "Good work," I say, trying to keep the relief out of my voice. I always knew she and Caesar could fix Junie's app, but knowing and seeing are different. The relief is palpable, like the first drop of rain after a long drought.

Sarah steps closer, her eyes locking onto mine. "But

there's something else you should know. Junie had to sell her grandmother's wedding ring to settle some debts."

"I know." The air grows heavy, almost stifling. I can feel her words press down on me like a boulder on my chest. I'd been that debt. My fingers tighten around the armrest of my chair, nails digging into the leather as if seeking stability in a turbulent sea.

"What will you do about it?" she asks, a delicate challenge lingering in her voice.

"I don't even know which pawn shop it is," I murmur, my mind racing, wondering how long it would take me to call every shop in town. "If I did, I'd do something about it."

"It's the one near Saks. I looked it up, and it's called Maxfield something or another."

The information hits me with the force of a freight train. For a moment, I can only stare at Sarah, trying to digest the news. She shrugs as if to say, "Your move," before turning on her heels and leaving my office. The door clicks shut behind her, but her words hang heavy in the room.

I spend the next hour fidgeting in my chair, staring at the phone on my desk. I should be doing a dozen other things—answering emails, reviewing contracts, preparing for upcoming meetings. Yet all I can do is sit there, half-expecting, half-hoping for a notification from Love Bug to light up my screen. Time stretches and compresses, warping around my thoughts. What could Junie be doing right now? Is she okay? Does she hate me?

Eventually, I can't stand it any longer. Pushing back

my chair, I grab my coat and phone, and stride out of my office. I don't even bother to tell anyone where I'm going. It's not like they would understand. The elevator ride down feels excruciatingly slow, each floor passing like a minor eternity. When the doors finally slide open, I rush out into the crisp evening air.

It takes me less than fifteen minutes to reach the pawn shop near Saks, but when I get there, I find it closed. The metal gate is down, and through the bars, I can see the rows of watches, guitars, and other items—each one a story of desperation or need. My fists clench, a rush of emotions battling within me. Frustration at myself for not getting here sooner, anger at the world for putting her in this situation, and a sharp, gut-wrenching fear that I've lost something invaluable, something that no amount of money can buy back.

I'm standing there, staring through the gate, lost in my thoughts, when a familiar voice shatters the silence.

"AJ? What on Earth are you doing here?"

I turn to find my mother standing there, her eyes wide. Dressed in her elegant cashmere coat and adorned with tasteful jewelry, she looks like she's just stepped out of a high-end social event—entirely at odds with the gritty surroundings of the locked-up pawn shop and the evening's invading darkness.

For a moment, I'm at a loss for words. How could I explain to her what led me here? How could she understand this desperate, clawing need to set things right? And as I stand there, caught in my mother's questioning gaze, I wonder if I'll ever find the right words to explain it all—not just to her, but to myself.

"Have you eaten, Mom?" I ask, realizing the late hour and the questions in her eyes.

"No, I haven't," she admits.

"How about dinner at Historic John's Grill? We can catch up."

A small smile warms her features. "That sounds lovely."

We walk several blocks and enter the restaurant. The ambiance surrounds us like a cozy, nostalgic blanket. The dark wood paneling and vintage photos on the walls evoke a bygone era, while the hum of low conversation mixed with clinking glasses lends the place an air of subtle elegance. Waitstaff glide through the room with practiced grace, adding to the restaurant's welcoming atmosphere.

We're led to a secluded booth, its high back providing a sense of intimacy amid the ambient bustle. Menus are handed to us, and my mother flips hers open, perusing the wine selection with an air of discernment.

"Would you like to choose the wine?" she asks, looking up from her menu.

"Certainly," I reply, eager to contribute to the mood of the evening. I opt for a bottle of Cabernet Sauvignon, known for its robust character—somewhat akin to the complexities I'm navigating in my own life. As the waiter uncorks the bottle and pours a small amount for me to taste, my mother's eyes catch mine.

"Do you think we should invite Junie?" she asks as the waiter fills our glasses.

A strange sensation washes over me, a blend of panic and introspection. My mother's innocent question cuts to the core of the tangled web of emotions, deceptions, and true feelings that have complicated my relationship with Junie.

Taking a sip of wine, I allow its rich flavor to distract me momentarily. Finally, I set down the glass and look into my mother's eyes, grounding myself in their maternal warmth.

"Mom, Junie and I aren't a couple. It was all a ruse."

She laughs. "Is that what you think? You can lie to yourself, but I know what I saw."

My mother's eyes are far keener than I give her credit for. "Mom, this whole charade was meant to distract you from playing matchmaker. But then, when I was around Junie and saw her passion and sincerity, I realized it wasn't a charade for me anymore. She's authentic in a way I've rarely seen." I tell my mother everything.

My mother narrows her eyes, studying me like she's decoding a complex equation. "So, you started this to deceive me but ended up deceiving yourself into some-thing genuine?"

"Surprisingly, yes. I found something real when I wasn't even looking," I admit, finally verbalizing the transformation that had been so difficult to understand myself.

My mother's eyes shine. "AJ," she begins, her voice imbued with an emotional resonance that I've seldom heard, "you don't have to explain yourself to me. Sometimes, the heart has its reasons where reason knows not. What I saw between you and Junie couldn't be faked, not by the best actor in the world. You need to make sure she knows how you feel."

We order and eat, and the air grows heavier as we sit in a bubble of silence and drink the last of the wine. With the taste of Cabernet still fresh on my lips, I find myself wrestling with my mother's counsel and my own misgivings.

"Why did you push me toward alliances built on money and status?"

My mother's eyes lock onto mine, penetrating layers of doubt and confusion. She sets her glass down, takes a deep breath, and opens a chapter of candid vulnerability that's rare between us.

"Do you think I paraded all those vapid debutantes around because I thought they were right for you?" She shakes her head, a wistful smile painting her lips. "AJ, it was all a ruse, but not in the way you're thinking. I showcased what you shouldn't want, hoping you'd recognize what you should want when you saw it. Sometimes, the quickest way to find the light is to sift through the darkness."

For a moment, I'm taken aback by her admission. All those staged dinners and awkward encounters were her twisted but loving way of guiding me toward authenticity. I had misunderstood her intentions as an endorsement of shallowness when, in fact, she was attempting to set the stage for something real.

Suddenly, my mother reaches across the table and grips my hand, her touch gentle yet full of a mother's wisdom.

"Don't be afraid to live outside of ledgers and contracts. The most precious assets aren't quantifiable. And Junie, she's a once-in-a-lifetime kind of investment," she says, the gravity of her words sinking deep into the marrow of my being.

The room around us seems to fade into a soft blur, the clinking glasses and hushed conversations melting away. All that remains is this moment of truth, a sliver of time suspended between a past I can't change and a future I'm just starting to envision.

"Thank you, Mom," I whisper, realizing that her intricate lessons and my circuitous journey have brought me here to this juncture between love and choice. "I think I finally understand."

Our glasses clink in a toast, a mutual acknowledgment that the journey ahead is one neither of us can foresee, but both of us will cherish. Tomorrow, there will be a pawn shop to visit, a ring to reclaim, and a woman to win over, not through schemes but through the genuine language of the heart.

CHAPTER TWENTY-SEVEN

JUNIE

The remote control feels cold in my hand as I cycle through an endless parade of sappy romantic comedies. Nope. Can't do it. Not today. I finally land on *Alone,* a reality show that drops people into isolated wilderness to see how long they can survive.

"Would I last an hour or a day?" I muse, engrossed in the scene of a contestant struggling to set up a makeshift tent. My thoughts drift toward the deeper notion of solitude, which starts in your gut and works its way into every corner of your life. I've never been great with metaphors, but if this isn't a reflection of my emotional state, I don't know what is.

A sequence of firm knocks interrupts my spiraling thoughts, snapping me back to the here and now. Hauling myself off the couch, I stride to the door and swing it open. Maxine Steel stands in the doorway, an epitome of elegance in her Chanel blouse and tailored trousers, pearls draped over her collarbone.

"What are you doing here? How do you know where I live?" My questions tumble out in a burst of genuine surprise.

Maxine's eyes dance with mischief. "I can afford spy shit, darling," she says.

My jaw drops, and I can't help but chuckle. "Well, when you put it like that. But really, what brings you here?"

"Lunch?" she offers. "I'd recommend wearing those bedazzled sneakers you love so much. Comfort before class, as they say."

I glance at my feet, adorned in fuzzy bunny slippers, and then back at Maxine. For a woman I've met only a few times, she's astonishingly perceptive.

"Alright," I agree, inviting her inside to wait, as I slip into my cherished bedazzled tennis shoes and a casual floral dress, comfort merging with a dash of flair. When I reemerge, Maxine eyes my footwear approvingly.

"Perfect," she says, and with a shared smile, we head out for a lunch that promises more than just food.

As we settle into a cozy bistro, the atmosphere is thick with the inviting scents of garlic and freshly baked bread. A vaulted ceiling opens above us, and warm, mellow lighting casts a golden glow over intricately patterned tablecloths and vintage wooden chairs. This is one of those exclusive hideaways where entry isn't so much about reservations but who you know. And Maxine, with her impeccable style and connections, clearly knows everyone.

Gently, the waiter places two flutes of champagne

before us, bubbles racing to the top as if vying for Maxine's attention. Her fingers, adorned with tastefully delicate rings, lift the flute elegantly. "To surprises," she declares, her eyes glittering like the jewels she wears.

I consider her toast and then raise my own glass. "To uncertainty," I reply, the clear ring of our flutes tapping together and filling the air.

We both take a sip, the champagne effervescent on my tongue. Maxine sets her glass down gently, and her gaze, insightful and just a little piercing, meets mine. "Junie, I genuinely want my son to find happiness. You might not believe me, but the glow that emanates from him when you're in the room? It's unmistakable. I can't remember the last time I saw him so ... alive."

Her words catch me off guard, and I almost cough out my champagne. I manage to swallow before blurting, "Really? Even when someone like Camilla is a more appropriate match?"

Maxine's laugh is sophisticated yet genuine, and I have to wonder if it's natural or something she learned in finishing school. "Camilla? That woman is as satisfying as a spoonful of plain oatmeal—perfectly adequate but utterly forgettable. Junie, you're crème brûlée—complex, with unexpected depths, and a bit of fire under that sweetness."

I feel my cheeks flush with both embarrassment and delight. There's something heartening about hearing it from Maxine, the woman who birthed the man whose love I'm still uncertain of. Perhaps there's more substance to this thing between AJ and me than I'd allowed myself to believe. And if that's coming from Maxine, it can't be entirely off the mark.

The waiter approaches our table, a crisp linen cloth draped over his arm. "Are we ready to order?" he asks, his eyes shifting between Maxine and me.

"Grilled octopus for the table," Maxine announces, returning the menu to the waiter. "And I'll have the lobster bisque. It's the best in the city." She looks at me. "You should give it a whirl."

My eyes widen. "Only if you want to kill me. I'm allergic to shellfish."

Maxine arches an eyebrow. "Darling, if I wanted you dead, I wouldn't go through the menu. I can afford people for that, too."

"In that case," I say, glancing at the waiter, "I'll settle for the beet salad. Less life-threatening and no need for espionage."

As the waiter retreats, Maxine leans in, resting her elegantly manicured hands on the table. "Shall we talk about what's really important?"

I nod, knowing that the conversation was never meant to be about sparkly shoes or for-hire assassins. "I'm all ears."

"AJ loves you."

The words encircle my heart and squeeze. "Impossible."

"Junie, AJ may have the relationship IQ of a stone, but trust me, he's willing to learn. Willing to try. Willing to evolve."

I chuckle at her blunt assessment. "Really? Because from where I'm standing, he's got a long way to go."

"That's where you come in. You are what AJ desires." Maxine grins. "Think of yourself as a rare gem. Not quite a pink diamond, mind you. Let's not make it impossible for the poor boy. But something like an alexandrite—complex, shifting, requiring the right light to truly shine. AJ can be your light."

I consider her words, weighing them against the man who broke my heart. "I am not a priceless stone coveted by the world."

"He believes you are." Maxine gazes into my eyes, searching for something only she knows. "More importantly though, you have to believe it. Set the standard for how people treat you. Don't be a pearl when you can be a diamond."

Our food arrives, but I consider Maxine's words. We share smiles as we indulge in our chosen dishes, savoring each bite as if acknowledging that life, too, is to be relished.

After the last spoonfuls and forkfuls are consumed, Maxine pats her lips with her napkin and says, "Care for a shopping detour before we part ways?"

Piqued, I nod. "Sure, why not?"

We head to Neiman Marcus and go directly to the shoe department, where Maxine asks for a pair of Golden Goose Superstars in a size seven. The sales associate returns promptly, presenting the bedazzled sneakers with a flair befitting their $685 price tag. Maxine immediately puts them on.

I can't believe she'd pay that for sneakers. I could have glued some rhinestones on Vans and saved her a bundle.

Maxine hands over her credit card to the cashier as if she's buying a latte when the total of her purchase would feed me for two weeks at least—a whole month if I stuck to Top Ramen and Kombucha. She grabs the bag containing her old shoes and marches toward the door in her new kicks.

"Life's too short for regrets," Maxine says, catching my eye. "If it brings you joy and it's within your means, then why not?"

"I guess some would argue it's an extravagance," I say cautiously.

Maxine smiles, her newly purchased bedazzled sneakers glittering as she moves. "Extravagance is in the eye of the beholder, darling. These," she says, pointing to her feet, "are an investment in a new perspective. Your perspective." She gives me a hug and an air kiss on both cheeks before she exits the store. "Never forget to shine, Junie." She turns and walks in the opposite direction.

Her words and the investment she's made to understand me pull me into a moment of introspection. If Maxine—the grand dame of decorum and paragon of high society—believes I'm worth understanding, perhaps I need to readjust how I value myself.

As I'm lost in thought, I pass by the pawn shop where I sold my grandmother's ring. A whimsical idea flashes across my mind. Maybe I should visit the ring, you know, like divorced parents sharing custody. Chuckling at my ridiculousness, I open the shop door and approach the counter.

"Hi, I'm here for visitation rights with my grandmother's wedding set?" The shopkeeper gives me a puzzled look before realizing what I mean. He shuffles over to the display case and then looks up, a regretful expression clouding his face.

"Ah, sorry, Miss. The ring has found a new home."

My heart sinks a little, but I manage a small smile. "Well, I hope it's happy in its new life."

I step out of the pawn shop, my emotions teetering on the edge. As I descend into the transit station, I'm wrapped in a cocoon of my own turmoil, despite the buzz of commuters. The train itself offers a rhythmic solace, a chance to reflect as the world zips by in a blur.

At the designated station, I surface back into the daylight, the city's rhythm pulsating around me. I locate the bus stop, where the route to Tiburon awaits. The bus ride is less of a solace and more of a bridge between two worlds - the urban hustle and the serene, almost introspective tranquility of Tiburon.

As the bus winds its way, the scenery shifts, marking my transition not just in space, but in mindset. Stepping off in Tiburon, I head toward home.

As I turn the corner onto my street, I'm met with a sight so bewildering, I actually stop to rub my eyes. My entryway has flowers everywhere. We're talking roses, tulips, lilies, daisies. It's like the Garden of Eden decided to hold a yard sale on my doorstep.

My first thought? *Oh, dear. Did old Mrs. Clark from*

the third floor finally die? I step closer, half-expecting to see an array of condolence cards.

But as I pluck a small card wedged amid the foliage, I read, "Because you're more captivating than any flower." It's signed with the initials AJ and scribbled with a heart. Every single botanical explosion of color and scent is for me, from AJ.

The absurdity of it all bubbles up into a laugh that echoes down the hallway. Here I am, worrying about pawned rings and lost heirlooms, and life just throws a full-blown flower shop at my feet.

Any lingering sadness about the ring eases, replaced by a sense of wonder and a feeling of being deeply cherished. In that moment, I realize that while some treasures can be pawned, others grow in value with each passing second, blooming in places you least expect.

Suddenly, Maxine's words echo in my mind. *Extravagance is in the eye of the beholder.*

And as I stand there, surrounded by enough flora to jump-start my own flower shop, I think to myself, maybe it's time to stop undervaluing me. Perhaps the solitary wilderness I often find myself in is self-imposed. Maybe, just maybe, I am crème brûlée in a world full of oatmeal, and I should start believing it.

CHAPTER TWENTY-EIGHT

AJ

I pace the floor of my office, a high-rise refuge that feels more like a prison today. Usually a fortress for my focus and decision-making, the space now serves as a chamber for my doubts. My desk, once a sanctuary, remains indifferent to my turmoil.

The clock on the wall taunts me, stretching each second into an endless loop of what-ifs. Has she seen the flowers? Were they too much or not enough? In the selection I sent, was one her favorite? Or maybe her floral tastes are as quirky as she is. Perhaps I should have sent a bacon bouquet. Does she hate flowers and prefer something like succulents? The word succulent makes me think of her lips, breasts, and the space between her thighs that I want to explore. Now I'm back to pacing, only this time aroused and uncomfortable as my boxers chafe my skin. The discomfort is a tiny scolding, telling me what a fool I was to let her go without saying the three words that scream inside me.

Declaring them now would feel cheap, as if my love for her was an afterthought. But it's not. It's a truth so intense, so vital, it feels like the core of me—something I must express, but only at a time that does justice to the moment.

When I think I can't wait another second, my phone vibrates. Anticipation surges through me, but the screen displays not her name but a notification from the dating app. A new challenge? My impatience shifts to relief. This app has led me to her and guided me this far. It feels like a compass pointing to Junie.

The screen glows with the next challenge.

Create a memory that will last a lifetime. Meet at Powell Street cable car turnaround tomorrow at 3 p.m.

Relief floods through me. Until now, the app's challenges have been a mixed bag of excitement and anxiety. But this? This is a lifeline. It gives me a path forward, an action I can take to close the gap between me and Junie.

My thoughts drift to tomorrow. What will I wear? I've always been a suit guy—tailored jackets, crisp shirts, the whole nine yards. It's a style that screams stability, professionalism, and a dash of traditionalism. But as I think about Junie, even my typical casual dress doesn't feel right. This isn't a business meeting or lunch at the club. It's a date etched into the fabric of everyday life, punctuated by the rumbling of cable cars and the hum of the city. The thought sends a shiver of excitement through me. Is this the moment to step out of my comfort zone? To let down my guard a little and show a side of me that's less polished, more relaxed?

The idea feels both unsettling and exhilarating. For tomorrow, a suit might represent the old me, while something as simple yet intentional as a graphic tee could symbolize a shift. Besides, I know Junie would appreciate the effort, the gesture of donning something so out of character for her sake.

There it is. My decision's made. Tomorrow, I won't be in my usual Brooks Brothers or Armani uniform. I'll be the guy in the funny, quirky T-shirt bound to light her eyes.

My phone remains mute. Still no word from her. But with this newfound clarity about tomorrow, that silence seems less intimidating. The app's challenge has ignited something within me, a spark evolving into a flame of determination.

I tap "Accept" on the app with renewed hope. A surge of anticipation fills me. Tomorrow is a new beginning, not just for me but, I hope, for both of us. And that, in itself, is already shaping up to be a memory worth holding onto.

THE MORNING LIGHT filters through the blinds, casting a warm glow over my room. Today is the day, and I can't help but feel a mix of excitement and nerves. I've set the stage with flowers. Now it's time for Act Two.

Last night, I got on Amazon and ordered a shirt with

same-day delivery. Slipping into the shirt, I feel like I'm donning a new identity, embracing a side of me waiting for the right moment to emerge. But I don't stop there. Along with my graphic tee, I choose a pair of casual jeans and some comfortable sneakers, finishing the look with a worn-in leather jacket that gives off an air of relaxed confidence.

Before heading out, I make one last stop—a small café where they make these incredible raspberry macarons that I'm sure Junie will love. I grab a box, thinking they'd be a sweet touch to our cable car ride. It's a small detail, but the small details make a memory last, right?

Arriving at the Powell Street cable car turnaround, my heart rate picks up. The area buzzes with tourists and locals alike. I check my watch. It's almost 3 p.m.

No sign of her yet. A flicker of doubt crosses my mind, but I push it away. I stand there, a box of macarons in one hand, the other in my jacket pocket, waiting for her to step into the frame of this picture-perfect moment I've set up in my mind.

Minutes tick by, but they feel like hours. I can't help but wonder if Junie will show, if she's as invested in us, or if I ruined it all. I look at all approaching cars, seeing if the red-headed girl I adore is riding in any of them. I recheck my watch, the time glaring back at me—3:24. A knot of disappointment tightens in my stomach. My fingers itch to reach for my phone, but I resist. There's no point in calling. She didn't show, and she has her reasons. The macarons are still in my hand, now feeling like a foolish token.

"Last call!" The operator's voice breaks through my thoughts.

Making a snap decision, I step into the car. It's not the outcome I'd hoped for, but maybe a solo ride will provide clarity and help me figure out my next move. As the car gains momentum, my thoughts blur with the scenery.

Just then, another cable car approaches from the opposite direction. I glance up, and for a split second, our eyes meet. It's her—Junie.

We react at the exact same moment, dashing toward the back of our respective cars.

"I'm sorry I'm late," she yells.

As our cable cars move away from each other, the gap between us gets bigger. I feel like I can't let that happen again. I launch myself over the rear railing. My feet pound the pavement as I race after Junie's car. My *Notting Hill*-themed shirt clings to me as I make the mad dash. The fabric, adorned with the phrase "I'm just a boy, standing in front of a girl," flutters against the wind. Catching the car and hoisting myself aboard, I see her eyes widen in recognition—not just at me, but at the shirt. Her laughter rings out, a joyful sound that slices through the noise of the cable car's clattering and the tourists' excited chatter.

Ignoring the conductor's grumbled complaints about fares and regulations, I sweep Junie into my arms, lifting her off her feet. "Better late than never." As our lips meet, I can't help but think, this is it, the memory we were meant to create. And as I hold her, wearing a shirt I knew would make her laugh and clutching the macarons I'd bought just for her, I realize that sometimes, the universe has a funny way of making things work out.

"I'm so glad you showed up. I couldn't imagine another challenge without you there," I say as I set her back on her feet, unwilling to break the contact between us.

Junie's eyes sparkle with mischief. "Oh, I tried to make it to Alcatraz, but a seagull staged an attack. Nearly amputated my finger."

I chuckle, my heart lighter than it's been in days. "So, you didn't cut it while slicing a bagel?"

"No, I nearly lost it feeding Cheetos to an angry bird."

Like that, every ounce of uncertainty melts away, replaced by a joy so pure that it could only mean one thing—we're exactly where we're meant to be. "I love you, Junie." As if words were not enough, I show her how much with another kiss.

Then someone yells, "Get a room!"

Junie turns to me, her eyes shining, and says, "I think that's a brilliant idea."

JUNIE

My lips are barely an inch away from AJ's as the cable car slows to a stop. Every part of me screams to be closer to him, yet a sliver of practicality interrupts the magnetic pull. "We need to go somewhere private."

AJ looks at me, eyes clouded with the same urgency flooding my veins. "Your place?"

I laugh, a little breathless. "Tiburon. Too far."

He hesitates for a split second. "What about my place? It's right above the office."

I grin, "Closer. Definitely closer." As if on cue, our mouths crash together again, a tangle of need and redis-covery, and in between kisses, he tells me he's sorry and he's an idiot, and I accept both.

We stumble off the cable car, still wrapped around each other, and hail a cab. I can't keep my hands off him. He seems to share my struggle.

The cab driver glances at us in the rearview mirror,

his eyes wide. AJ notices and chuckles. "Keep your eyes on the road, buddy."

The driver rolls his eyes but complies, muttering something about "young love" under his breath. I can't help but giggle.

AJ pulls me closer, capturing my mouth with a deep kiss that makes me dizzy. I forget about the cab, the driver, the road—all that matters is the electric charge between us. For a moment, the world narrows to this small, intimate space where the chemistry is so palpable that it feels like a third passenger in the car.

Finally, the cab screeches to a halt in front of AJ's building. A wave of relief washes over me. The waiting is over, and the promise of what's to come sends a thrill down my spine.

He tosses some bills to the driver, not even bothering to check the amount. "We're here," he whispers.

"Finally," I reply, the word coming out as a sigh of relief.

Caught in the pull of each other's gravity, we stumble into his private elevator, and when the door opens, we practically trip over our feet as we navigate blindly through the room. Our lips remain locked, our hands exploring new landscapes, and it's as though we've left the world behind.

It's only when my back gently hits the smooth surface of AJ's desk that we both pause, realizing where we've ended up.

"Your office?" I question, my eyebrows lifting in surprise.

"Seems so. I just pushed the button. Habit, I guess. It's where I spend most of my life." He chuckles, a mischievous gleam lighting up his face. "And I'm suddenly very okay with wherever we are as long as we're together."

With a sweep of his arm, the trappings of corporate life that clutter his desk are sent flying—a hailstorm of papers, the expulsion of a stapler, and even a potted plant that, quite frankly, has seen better days. Now clear, the desk surface suddenly feels like a realm of infinite possibilities.

He hoists me onto it, our eyes locking as if asking silent permission. "Can't wait," he confesses, the words a low rumble that stirs the air between us.

The paperwork will wait. The emails, calls, and responsibilities that usually bind him to this desk will be there tomorrow. But today, this room, generally reserved for meetings and strategy sessions, serves as the setting for a different kind of merger.

"Why seek another floor?" I pull him closer, my eyes meeting his. "When my world is right here?"

The door creaks open just as our lips are about to meet again. A surprised gasp interrupts us, and AJ's assistant sticks her head in, eyes widening at the scene before her.

"Oh! I-I thought I heard something." Her cheeks flush with embarrassment. "My apologies."

"Out!" AJ and I yell in unison, so perfectly synced that it would be comedic under different circumstances.

With another squeak and a hurried nod, Miss Clark hastily withdraws, pulling the door shut behind her.

We stare at each other for a split second, caught somewhere between hilarity and urgency. Then AJ smirks and says, "I'll make sure to put a Do Not Disturb sign up next time."

Knowing he's already thinking about our future makes my heart feel full. "Or just lock the door," I suggest.

"Even better," he says.

As if drawn by magnets, our lips find each other again. The door to the outside world is firmly shut. All hesitance and doubt vanish as our desire for one another overwhelms us.

Here, on this desk, we shut out the outside world to settle into the truth that we are irresistibly drawn to each other. No one and nothing can take away from this powerful connection.

In a room where numbers and algorithms reign supreme, we create something that transcends data and speaks from our hearts. It is an experience that is hard to quantify, yet it permanently marks our souls. It's not about logic or reason. It's simply about love.

He presses me into the edge of the desk, his hands tracing the contours of my waist before settling at my hips. The intensity of his gaze sears through me. His eyes are smoldering, brimming with unbridled lust, and I can feel my heart rate increasing in response. I allow myself a moment to take in every inch of him. The broadness of his shoulders, the narrowing of his waist, the sheer beauty of him standing before me in that graphic T-shirt I love so much.

We move together without speaking, as if under some kind of spell. His hands are everywhere, sending shivers through my entire body with each touch. Feeling daring, I slide mine beneath his clothes to explore further and feel his response. His breath grows raspier as he loses himself completely when I grip his length.

Our clothes fall away, and it's just him and me, our bodies pressing harder against one another as we explore each other intimately. Our movements become urgent as pleasure dominates our senses until we are both consumed with need.

"I can't wait any more." He points to his pants. "Do we need a condom?"

I shake my head. I don't want another thing coming between us. "No, I'm on birth control."

"Thank God."

A relieved sigh escapes him as his hands take hold of my hips and draw me closer. His fingertips graze the small of my back, and I feel my body melting into his embrace.

He enters me slowly and steadily until I am filled with nothing but him. With each movement, our bodies adopt a rhythm like two parts of the same machine. Our breath grows faster as pleasure consumes us. This isn't just sex. It's something far more—a union of two people, not just in body but in purpose. It's a silent pledge, an unspoken vow that says, "I see you, not just for who you are, but for who we could be together."

The intensity of our connection is so strong that I can't help but gasp out loud when he hits the right spot—and he's skilled in hitting that spot. It's like nothing else exists in the world. My desire for him swells until he's ripping the climax from me.

I try to keep my voice low, but moments later, a moan escapes my lips as I give in entirely to pleasure. That is all he needs. He pushes us both over the edge and into pure ecstasy with one final thrust.

We lay there afterward in a blissful trance, him draped over my naked body, enjoying every second of being together without having to say a word. As his lips meet mine, it's as if he's sealing my broken parts back together, one kiss at a time. Every caress becomes a cornerstone in the sanctuary we're building, filled with love and promise.

And in that room where my dreams were once ripped apart, a new dream takes root, nurtured by the newfound understanding that home isn't a place. It's a feeling, a moment, a person. Home is with AJ.

He helps me dress and leads me to the elevator. "Let's order food, watch *Notting Hill*, and make love again."

We step into the empty elevator to move to his place one floor up. As the elevator doors glide open, I step into his penthouse for the first time, my eyes widening. It's a masterpiece of modern elegance—black, gray, white, and silver dominating every inch of space, from the sleek furniture to the abstract art on the walls. It's breathtaking but also a bit sterile, like a photo from a design magazine rather than a home.

"Do you have something against color?" I tease, glancing around the monochrome space.

He laughs, pulling me closer into the expansive living area. "I was thinking about getting an orange cable-knit throw and some ridiculously bright pink pillows."

My face brightens, and I can't help but smile. "You're in luck. I know just the place to get them. Sounds like my living room is about to clone itself here."

He grins, the smile reaching his eyes, making them twinkle. "Then it would truly feel like home."

The energy between us is like a warm current that seems to flow seamlessly from one to the other. For a moment, we stand there, basking in the reality of us, a reality neither thought possible a few short days ago.

Pulling away slightly, AJ gestures toward a stylish sectional. "How about we start with that food order and see where the evening takes us?"

AJ

As the credits of *Notting Hill* roll on the screen, I hit the mute button on the remote and set it aside. The laughter and banter we shared during the movie still echo in the room, filling the space with joy. Junie snuggles closer, the warmth of her body melding into mine as her head finds its place on my chest.

"So, what do you think?" she asks, her voice tinged with a soft curiosity. "Hugh Grant's character owns a bookshop, and Julia Roberts is this mega movie star. If that were us, if you were just a guy who runs a multimillion-dollar tech firm, and I'm—well, me—would we make it?"

Weeks ago, I might have hesitated, dissected the logic, and calculated the risks. But that was a different me, untouched by the transformative power of love.

My arms tighten around her, pulling her closer. "I used to think love was a luxury I couldn't afford, a distraction from the relentless push for success," I confess, my voice layered with newfound understanding. "But I've realized love isn't about balancing spreadsheets or merging assets. It's about merging hearts, building a life together, out of respect, trust, and commitment."

She tilts her head back to look up at me, her eyes searching my face as if trying to map the terrain of my soul. "So, you think we'd make it?"

"With you, I'm rediscovering a world of possibilities I'd written off long ago," I say, brushing a strand of hair from her face. "So, yeah, I think we'd more than make it. We'd thrive in our own unconventional, incredible way."

Junie pauses, her expression turning thoughtful, perhaps a little anxious. "But let's be real, AJ. I'm poor, and you're—"

"Rich beyond measure," I interrupt, locking eyes with her. "And do you know why? It's not because of my bank account. It's because you saw through my shortsightedness and loved me despite my flaws. That makes me the richest man on earth."

She chuckles, but I see the skepticism lingering in her eyes.

"You're not poor, Junie," I continue, taking out my phone. "Have you looked at the numbers lately?"

Shaking her head, she sighs. "After Sarah and Caesar left my apartment, I forgot the password they gave me. I haven't checked."

With a few taps, I access the analytics for her app. My eyes widen at the numbers before showing her the screen.

"Take a look. You're wealthy in your own right. This is your doing. Your vision has come to life."

Her eyes scan the figures, disbelief settling in. "Is that ... How much can an app make in a day?"

"Reviews are great, and buys are up by 150%. You've built something incredible here," I say, unable to keep the pride out of my voice. "Even the people who gave negative reviews have gone back to amend their reviews after the app reset and provided them proper matches. And it turns out that that guy and his bingo-loving neighbor were a love match after all."

Junie looks at me, her eyes wide, but I see a shift in her gaze—like she's starting to see herself in a new light. It's like she's looking into a mirror, and it's reflecting back an image she hadn't dared to consider. "I didn't know it was doing that well."

"And it's just the start," I add, my voice tinged with a confident hope I haven't felt in a long time. "With the right moves, it could be even more profitable. But money aside, what's really valuable here is your creativity, insight, and resilience. You're not poor, Junie. You never were."

"I bet you regret kicking me out of the competition."

"Yes," I admit, my gaze never leaving hers. "I regret it, not because of business, but because it hurt us—hurt you. Rules are important, but they shouldn't ruin something good. And what do we have? It's beyond good."

She nods. "That's all I needed to hear."

As Junie embraces me, I feel like the wealthiest man in the world—and not because of the financial empire I've built. No, it's because of this incredible woman who sits beside me, full of life, love, and a richness that numbers could never capture.

"And you didn't think it was possible, did you? You didn't think my app could dig down in the deep recesses and find what mattered," she says softly, her gaze delving into mine.

"I was wrong," I admit, pulling her closer. Our lips meet in a kiss that feels like a silent vow. "We are perfectly matched."

Junie's lips curve into that smile that's come to mean the world to me—a smile that feels like home, like the promise of every tomorrow I ever want to see.

In this quiet moment, the enormity of what we've found hits me full force. This is no fleeting affair, no passing emotion. It's a cornerstone, a foundation for a future I hadn't dared to imagine until she walked into my life and turned every assumption upside down.

As she leans in, our lips a whisper apart, I sense the crossing of an invisible threshold. It's a point of no return, but the thought of turning back is unthinkable.

We're not just playing roles in a romantic film that's bound to end. This is our life, unscripted and uncertain but breathtakingly real. And that's the beauty of it—because love, in its truest form, needs no script. It writes its own story, one beautiful, flawed, perfect moment at a time.

The morning light seeps through the windows, painting our room in hues of liquid gold. As I walk to the bathroom to shower, my fingers graze the sumptuous texture of Egyptian cotton, a world away from my old flannel sheets.

The products on the shelf aren't dime-store-bought but pure luxury, as is the rain shower head above my head. It's all like living a dream, but this is no dream. This is my life. Once finished, I wrap a towel around myself and walk through the loft.

The once-sleek, minimalist space now hums with vibrant pieces of our combined lives. A cable-knit throw sprawls across the back of his modern sofa. Near a collection of AJ's abstract art hangs my proudly displayed posters featuring Jobs, Musk, and Winfrey, each looking contemplative and wise.

AJ, already dressed in his tailored suit, struggles with

his tie in front of the mirror. "Good morning," I say, my voice filled with cheerfulness.

"Morning," he replies, watching me in the mirror as I dress. "Another day in the empire?" he quips, a hint of playfulness touching his eyes.

Absolutely," I say, slipping into my blazer with a sense of purpose. "As the newly minted in-house therapist for Steel Enterprises, I'm on a mission to transform workplace stress into creative fuel." His eyes sparkle, and there's an unspoken understanding between us. "Although every time I try to de-stress you, I find myself happily on my back, on your office desk downstairs. It's a fascinating phenomenon, don't you think?"

"That desk has never seen so much action," he laughs.

I chuckle. "It's a multitasking marvel, much like us."

Helping him finish the tie with a neat knot, I marvel at how much my life has changed in thirty days. From my fledgling career to love as grounding as it is uplifting, every aspect feels transformed.

"We're pretty amazing together, aren't we?" he says, meeting my eyes.

"Amazing doesn't even begin to cover it." I flash him a grin.

"Just wait, I've got a surprise for you."

"Another bacon bouquet?"

He chuckles. "No, but I think you'll enjoy it."

"I can't wait. Ready to go?" I ask.

"Where you go, I'll follow," AJ replies, offering his

arm. Arm in arm, we reach the elevator that connects our home directly to Steel Enterprises below.

The elevator dings open, and we step into his office.

"Care for some coffee?" AJ asks.

"Yes." We take a slight detour to the modern, airy lounge, bypassing the familiar faces of employees who greet us—some wave, some nod, all smile. A sense of pride wells up inside me. Not only am I forging my own path here, but I'm doing it beside a man who respects and loves me for who I am. I brew a caramel macchiato, and AJ chooses a straightforward black coffee. As I stir in a bit of sugar, Sarah approaches.

"Junie, can I talk to you?"

"Of course," I say, waving goodbye to AJ as he heads to his office. Sarah and I walk to my own nearby space—a welcoming area filled with comfy chairs, warm tones, and diplomas that sometimes still surprise me when I read my own name on them.

At my desk, I listen to Sarah express her concerns about a project, and for the next ninety minutes, we devise a plan to help her implement a stress-free work environment for her team. A knock interrupts us. The door swings open, revealing AJ dressed in full ladybug attire, with antennae and tights. My hand comes to my mouth to stifle a laugh. "What in the world?" My laughter bubbles out, uncontrollable, and genuine. "You look ridiculous!"

"Ridiculously committed to keeping my word," he corrects, brandishing two bags as if they're treasure chests. "And ridiculously in love with you."

With a theatrical flourish, he hands one bag to Sarah. "For you, a gourmet chicken salad, lovingly garnished with organic micro greens."

Sarah takes the bag, eyeing AJ's ladybug ensemble with disbelief. "Well, lunch just got more interesting."

"And for you, my love," AJ declares, pivoting dramatically toward me. He extends the second bag. "A peanut butter and jelly sandwich paired with a sophisticated bag of Cheetos." His eyes twinkle with mischief. "I've conducted a thorough seagull risk assessment, and I'm pleased to report we are in a seagull-free zone."

I can't help but burst into laughter, clutching the bag to my chest as if it's a sacred artifact. "Oh, you've really outdone yourself. The PB&J and Cheetos? Gourmet dining at its finest. But what's with the ladybug getup?"

"I may or may not have lost a bet to Henry. Your app, while not an asset of Steel Enterprises, is the most successful launch in our history," he admits, attempting a casual shrug, though the antennae wobble comically with the motion.

"And you thought it would lose," Sarah says.

"That was before he believed in love." Junie hugs her lunch to her chest.

The room vibrates with an energy of unfiltered joy, a stark contrast to the sterile, corporate ambiance one might expect. It's as if we've rewritten the rules, turning the ordinary into the extraordinary.

It's a vivid reminder that life has a funny way of surprising you when you least expect it. And as I look at the man I love, standing in my office dressed as a ladybug, I know that surprises—wonderful, ludicrous surprises— are what I can look forward to for the rest of my life.

CHAPTER 32
AJ - SIX MONTHS LATER

My palms sweat as if they've sprung tiny leaks, and each breath feels like I'm sipping air through a straw. I pull out my phone and look at the display—6:28 p.m. Two more minutes until showtime. I've brokered deals that would make Wall Street blush and steered projects with more zeros than most people see in a lifetime. Yet, none of that holds a candle to the significance of this moment.

Glancing down, my feet are snug in a pair of Vans Convicts—Junie's favorite. There is no bedazzling, just the iconic sneakers that make this moment feel authentic —just like her. I have on a graphic T-shirt, but the message is hidden by my buttoned blazer. The big reveal happens only if she says yes.

Taking a fortifying gulp of air, I push open the door of the hotel's bar. The atmosphere oozes sophistication, dim lights casting muted shadows on polished wood and plush upholstery. But even in this dimness, Junie glows, a magnetic force I can't resist. She's wearing a simple dress that compliments her every curve, her skin reflecting the golden flecks of light that dance around the room.

"Hey," I murmur, closing the distance between us. I place her hand, soft and warm, in mine and take us back to the beginning. "I know you don't know me, but I need your help. Can you play along? My mom's on this marriage crusade for me. Can you pretend to be my girl-friend? I promise it'll be worth it."

Her laughter is a melodic sound, a joyous ripple in the air as she nods. "For you? Anything." She looks down at my shoes and shakes her head. "What's with the kicks, Romeo?"

"I heard they were the best." I help her from her seat. "Ready for dinner?"

She nods, and confident steps guide us to the adjoining restaurant, The Pampered Palate. At the entrance, a placard reads, "Closed for Private Function."

"Looks like they're closed. What about Thai?" She pivots like she's ready to leave.

I chuckle, nudging the door open with my shoulder. "Don't worry. I've got some pull around here."

As we step in, her eyes widen. All around, our world comes to life. The gleaming chandeliers cascade light onto my mother, Liv, Henry, and every last person from the Steel Enterprises staff. They all sport bedazzled Vans Convicts—each foot adorned like a mini galaxy of stars. A string quartet fills the air with soft music, their bows sliding over the strings, creating the playlist for our future, including the B sides.

"Surprise!" the crowd erupts in unison.

Junie looks disoriented, her mouth opening and closing as if struggling to find the words. "What on Earth is happening here?"

Leading her further into this fairy-tale setting, I guide her to a small, intimate table. It stands like an island in a sea of faces, crowned by flickering candles and a bouquet of her favorite blooms—which I now know are Gerbera daisies. Their bright colors seem to beam with happiness, as if they, too, are in on this monumental moment. The sight calms my nerves, each vibrant petal a reminder of the joy she brings into my life.

After helping her sit, I pull a small velvet box from my pocket and drop to one knee. When I open the box to reveal the ring, her eyes widen in disbelief. It's her grandmother's ring—a vintage beauty that she thought was lost forever.

"How?"

"I did what most men won't. I listened and asked for directions." I place the ring at the tip of her ring finger. "Junie, will you be the constant in my ever-changing equation, the forever loop in my code of life? Will you marry me?"

Time seems to pause, allowing her reaction to fill the room. Liv sidles up to Junie, whispering almost conspiratorially, "I can't believe I gave him to you."

Junie's eyes flit from Liv's back to me, flashing like twin emeralds. "I earned him," she says with conviction. A soft "Yes" escapes her lips as she pushes her finger into the ring.

Cheers erupt around us, and applause fills every

corner of the room. Standing up, a sense of peace envelops me. As I unbutton my blazer, I reveal a graphic T-shirt underneath that reads "Under New Management," with a caricature of Junie above it.

In the middle of this joyful chaos, ecstatic faces, and the intoxicating feeling of love in the air, I realize something amazing. I've found my forever, and forever couldn't possibly be long enough.

Need a little more Junie and AJ? Want to see the wedding? Go here https://BookHip.com/VXWNKSL and join my list.

Want to find out what kind of Love Bug you are? Take this fun quiz at https://www.jotform.com/form/232698043774163

ALSO BY KELLY COLLINS

Love Bug Novels

Swipe Right for Romance

The Dating Dilemma

An Aspen Cove Romance Series

One Hundred Reasons

One Hundred Heartbeats

One Hundred Wishes

One Hundred Promises

One Hundred Excuses

One Hundred Christmas Kisses

GET A FREE BOOK.

Go to www.authorkellycollins.com

ABOUT THE AUTHOR

International bestselling author of more than thirty novels, Kelly Collins writes with the intention of keeping love alive. Always a romantic, she blends real-life events with her vivid imagination to create characters and stories that lovers of contemporary romance, new adult, and romantic suspense will return to again and again.

For More Information
www.authorkellycollins.com
kelly@authorkellycollins.com